The Adventures of Nuno and Figo

The Strange Journey of Two Unlikely Friends

Thomas H Murray

CONTENTS

INTRODUCTION

Nuno is a part of the Iberian Lynx family that lives in Portugal. Others live in Spain. He and his kinfolk are on the critically endangered red list of the International Union for Conservation of Nature (IUCN) The IUCN was founded in 1964 and is the world's most comprehensive inventory of the global conservation status of biological species.

Twenty years ago, there were only about 100 individuals left, mainly because of the rapid decline of the rabbit population due to habitat loss and disease. Today, thanks to conservation and protection efforts, there are about 400 Iberian lynxes in the wild with 109 in Portugal. The male Quinde and female Quisquilla, who were born in captivity in 2019, were released into the wild on March 8, 2020.

Besides relating an incredible story, I want to raise awareness to the danger these beautiful animals are facing to survive. I will donate 10% of the proceeds from this book to the organizations that are dedicated to their survival. Organizations like the following: World Wildlife Fund (WWF), SOS Lynx, Iberlynx, Interreg, etc.

DEDICATION

I dedicate this adventure to Susana Felizardo, my muse and my Portuguese Terpse. Her love has given me happiness and peace in my troubled life. She has opened the inner world of Portugal to me and inspires me to reach for higher creative heights.

CHAPTER ONE

"Times are tough," Nuno's father sighed, sitting in the courtyard of his Portuguese country house, typical of Iberian lynxes. He was dining on grilled rabbit and vinho verde (green wine) with his mates. Everyone nodded as he complained how difficult it was to find rabbits these days. Used to be one a day was enough, but now the rabbits were so thin, they needed to catch two. Some days they went without eating any. Nuno's stomach agreed with a loud grumble.

One of Nuno's friends told them that his uncle, Tiago, returned home recently and talked of a land far away where the rabbits are fat, slow, and many. It was called California and could only be reached after a long and difficult passage in the freighter ships from Lisboa. Considering how difficult it would be to just get to Lisboa, those freighters might as well be spaceships to the moon. Everyone nodded at the idea, but without any conviction.

Later, with more vinho verde than rabbit in his stomach, Nuno sought out his friend's uncle and asked for details about this dreamland. Tiago had returned only to take care of his ailing parents, being the only surviving son, and anyway that is what lynxes do. Nuno, on the other hand, was one of six surviving sons, and the others would be better at taking care of their parents than him. Nuno was eager to hear more.

Tiago sat back on his haunches and started to relate his strange adventure to the young Nuno.

"Yes, the rabbits are exactly as you heard. It's not all easy living there. For example, there are other beasts of the forest you must be careful of: giant lynxes, called lions of the mountains, and dangerous dogs called coyotes. And the roads, Nuno, the roads! You must be very careful of them. There are far more cars than here. Crossing roads is extremely dangerous.

"There are many more people, too, but they are good people. Rather than trying to kill you, they may think you are a large homeless house cat and try to force you to be a part of their family of people. If you're careful, you can raid the large cans outside their houses that they fill every day with all manner of strange but tasty foods.

"Enough!" Nuno cried. "How do I get there?"

"It's a hard and dangerous path there. First, you must go to Lisboa."

"I know, everyone tells me, but they never tried the trip. How do I get there?"

"Go to the highest hill around here and smell the air. If you're attentive, you will catch a very strange smell, unlike anything else you know. Follow that smell for a week or more and you will arrive at a place you cannot imagine. But you better get used to it. It's a chaos of cars, people, buildings as big as mountains, and a lot more. But whatever you experience there, it is a much smaller version of what you'll find in California."

"I can do that, but how do I find the freighter ship that took you there?"

"When you find the city, go straight south until you arrive at a large river. Turn right and continue westward along the river until you find them floating there. They are the size of large hills. You can't miss them. Now, this is when you must be patient. There is one that has this symbol on its front side: California Dreaming. I have no idea what it means."

He drew the letters in the dirt. Nuno memorized them carefully. After a moment he told Tiago to continue.

"This ship only arrives once a month. So, the odds are you will have to wait about two weeks. During this time, you will have to raid the cans of food at night or catch a foul-tasting sleeping pigeon. You will not meet anything but birds. However, if people see you, you better run and hide. Instead of their homes, they will catch you and enslave you for their amusement in a park where many people come on the weekends to gawk at you. You will be emasculated and broken, pacing up and down in a cage all your waking hours.

"Now when this ship arrives, it will come to the edge of the river and spend a day or two loading and unloading things. This is your chance. You must get on without being seen. You can climb up the thick ropes that hold the ship to the river's edge. Inside is larger than most of our forests, but there are no trees there. Instead, there are many large metal boxes as big as the local farmers' houses. Once inside, you can hide easily."

"Okay, so far, except it sounds like I will be very hungry. I've never eaten out of a can before. What about on the ship itself? Are there rabbits there?"

"No rabbits, but you may find huge mice who are much more dangerous. At first, I thought they were more fun to play with before I shredded them for dinner. They are about the size of our rabbits, but they will bite back. Otherwise, you can find the people's food center by smell. But only move at night, hidden in the darkness and the shadows.

"The ship stops at many ports on the way to California. Each time the ship will stop for about a day or so, taking out some of the large metal boxes they carry deep inside and putting in different ones. If you leave the ship, do not leave for more than a few hours. The trip takes about three weeks to arrive there. It comes directly back to Lisboa, and that trip only takes a week, if you ever change your mind."

"Oh, I won't!"

"Once you arrive about three weeks later at a place called Long Beach, leave by the ropes, and go south with the ocean on your right, but again only move at night. You will know you are at the final port because they will remove all the metal boxes. Instead of pigeons, you can catch slightly better tasting seagulls, and there are many food cans along the beaches. Beaches are sandy stretches where the ocean meets the land.

"After about a week, you will find more trees and hills that will remind you of here. That is where you turn eastward. When you see land that looks like our Xisto, you have arrived. You will find plenty of space where rabbits, things called squirrels, many mice-like animals, and much better tasting birds can be found.

"You will find possible mates. They will have small ears and silly long tails, but don't let that offend you. They can be good companions, but poor hunters. You can have a family like I did. I'm sad I had to leave them behind. This journey can only be done alone.

"But if you do find them, you would have a ready-made family, though I expect they are all grown now. The wonderful mate I found there had grown to like us Latinos from the old country. She says we have more class than the local competition and we smell better."

"Wow, that may be a good idea. How would I find her?"

"Don't worry about that. She'll find you. She likes our natural perfume. Most of the females there are much smaller than us. Though they are fat, spoiled, and rich brats. At first, I could never decide whether I should love them or eat them. In the end, I decided to love them and eat the rabbits and squirrels. But my Little T is a big cat, twice as big as any of the others. Maybe her father was a lynx. Don't know. We didn't talk much. Never had to."

"OK, OK, already! I'm ready to go! Which hill should I go to catch the Lisboa smells?"

"Not so fast, youngster. You can't leave until we have a sending-off dinner party. Alberto and his friends caught a few hares. Tomorrow, we'll send you off, if not in style, then at least with a full stomach. I'll also prepare a sack of dried rabbit that should get you through any hungry patches."

Nuno thanked Tiago warmly and spent the remaining time getting his affairs in order. He explained everything to his parents. His father understood, but his mother cried the rest of the day. He tried to explain to her that he was already grown up and needed to find his own destiny, even if that took him to the other side of the world. It did not help.

That evening was a rare time when food was plenty. There was even plenty of vinho verde, because, as Tiago explained, he had happened to find several cases that fell off the back of a delivery truck. After the vinho verde came the singing. Nuno's mother sang many beautiful Fado songs of Alfama, songs of yearning for lost loved ones and lost homelands.

After a while, Nuno's father broke in to stop the sobbing. And with his friends, they sang the joyful Fandango, causing everyone to start dancing, and then finished the night with the lynx folk songs of Alentejo.

Being naturally nocturnal, everyone slept through the next day. As the sun sank in the sky, Tiago gave Nuno some last-minute advice and pointed him to the best mountain top to catch the Lisboa scent. With lots of hugs and kisses all around and more crying, Nuno finally started his long journey. It took him most of the rest of the night to reach the mountaintop, including taking the time to catch a careless rabbit.

As the sun rose, Nuno sniffed and sniffed. After a few hours, sure enough, a faint strange smell was discernible from the scent of pine trees and the local earth. He managed to catch another rabbit; with a full stomach, he found a place hidden out of the sun to sleep the rest of the day.

He awoke to a full moon and started his journey, following the scent that would lead him to his dream. It took him a week of running at night (lynxes only run, never walk) to reach the first concrete river with cars flowing through it like water. He headed directly south like Tiago told him, towards the great river.

Nuno found himself increasingly going through the backyards of houses. The first time he did this, he nearly jumped out of his skin. A large dog attacked him, barking crazily. Luckily, Nuno's instinct kicked in and one swipe of his claws across the dog's face sent it yelping and running for safety. The dogs were too big to eat, but Nuno often found interesting food left outside in dishes that he thankfully polished off. This helped him to conserve the dried rabbit meant for emergencies.

The closer he approached the river, the less green land there was to hide his movements. There were no signs of rabbits at all. Fortunately, he was a night beast in the world of day lovers. Instead of food in dishes, he started finding many metal boxes filled with things to eat. He never ate before any of what he found there, but a hungry stomach is famous for tolerating anything new. He found half-eaten grilled chickens and other strange meats. Most of what he found was inedible, but he usually could find enough to eat after searching half a dozen cans.

Nuno found that sleeping and hiding during the day more and more difficult. The day before he reached the river, he found a nice place under some bushes in a small city park. He always worried a bit that his snoring might alert nearby enemies. But luckily, he did not snore like his father. One could hear that for meters around. Despite this, he had an awfully close call.

Late afternoon, a dirty drunken man stumbled his way to the bushes where Nuno was hiding. He pulled down his pants and was about to relieve himself on top of Nuno. Nuno gave a low growl and bit him where the sun does not shine. The man leaped up, running, and falling with his pants held up by his hands, screaming "O Diabo mordeu-me! Ó meu Deus, prometo nunca mais beber de novo! [The Devil bit me! Oh, dear God, I promise I'll never drink again!]"

Luckily, no one paid any attention to a raving drunken man. Nuno finished the last hours of daylight, wary of any more crazies coming near. Later, before he left the park, he ate his first pigeon. It was not enough. But before he could catch a second, his stomach started to complain. He vowed he would not eat another pigeon unless he was starving.

Nuno reached the river that night and he turned right like Tiago told him. After another day hiding in a water drainage pipe and half a night running in the shadows, he reached the place where the huge ships were floating in the river and a few tied up at dock.

None of them had the symbols that Tiago showed him in the dirt. A few more metal boxes of random food and a day sleeping in another drainage pipe brought him to the next night. He searched, always staying out of sight for the ship with those strange symbols. He could not find it. A week like this passed by, and Nuno started to worry if Tiago had his story right. But on the tenth night, he saw it floating in the river. He did not eat or sleep for two days as he watched that ship, willing it to come to the dock. Three days of this and the ship did dock with the long ropes securing it, just as Tiago had said.

Nuno raided a few cans of random people food until he was no longer hungry. He hid in the night shadows and stared at the rope for hours. This was the moment he was waiting for. Once he climbed up that rope and entered the ship, there would be no turning back. He questioned himself and what he was about to do. He realized how crazy the idea was. Doubts and fears flooded his mind. He started to dwell on all the things that could go wrong.

Just as he was about to turn around and return home, he thought of everyone's reaction when they would see that he had given up. His adventurous courage would turn into laughter and ridicule the rest of his life. He knew exactly how mean lynxes could be. Before he could think anymore, his legs quickly leapt up the rope and hurried inside the ship.

CHAPTER TWO

The top deck was stacked with metal containers with many more stacked in the hold below, accessed by going down through a large dark opening in the top deck. This was a tramp container ship. Unlike most container ships that travelled directly between two large ports, the SS California Dreaming would visit many small ports on its way home to Long Beach, California. So, there was much empty space for more containers to be stacked from future stops in Casablanca, Morocco, Dakar, Senegal, Recipe, Brazil, Paramaribo, Suriname, Barranquilla, Colombia, and Puerto Vallarta, Mexico. The containers bound for Portugal from California were being removed and replaced with those bound for the US and the other destinations.

It being night, all the cranes and containers rested silently in the darkness. There was a lone light in the bridge where the night watch paid attention to any movement in the harbor. He walked along the deck a few times with his flashlight during his six hours on duty. He was easy to avoid. Nuno jumped down into the hold by landing on the top of containers stacked at various heights. He had to explore this huge ship and find a place to hide during the day. He also had to find a source of food. He was fine for now, not having touched his emergency supply of dried rabbit, but he still had a long journey ahead of him.

The containers were stacked somewhat unevenly with plenty of space between them for a lynx to easily fit and hide. No one ever walked around there except to help with loading and unloading of containers. The hiding part was easy. Nuno was glad that this was not one of those ships carrying hundreds of people that he saw going further up the river. It was much easier to avoid the attention of sleeping metal containers and the few sailors who mainly cared about what was near or approaching the ship rather than a ship full of drunken people walking about at all hours of the night and day.

In the still night air, smelling something that might be a source of food, Nuno followed it towards the back of the ship where the slightly lit bridge rose above the deck. This seemed to be where the people lived and ate. There was a door with a round window at the base of this tower, but it was locked tightly. Nuno would have to return to the deck to find other entrances.

As he turned to make his way back up through the hole to the deck, something in the corner of his eye made him freeze. Something moved in the shadows. He sniffed and an offensive, almost evil smell worked its way into his nostrils through all the other smells of old lubricants and paint. It was the smell of a strange animal he had never met before. Was it a threat or food? Was it one of the rat things that Tiago told him about? He had to find out.

He crouched down low to the metal floor and slowly worked his way toward the ratty smell. Oh, how he wanted to growl! But he suppressed the urge. He inched closer to his prey. For about half an hour, he patiently crept closer until he came around a container and in the pale moonlight, made out a small, nervous black shadow.

As Nuno was about to attack, the rodent stood up on its hind legs and started a high-pitched squeaking. What a horrid sound! Just as Nuno was about to pounce on this obnoxious thing, something totally unexpected happened. The grey shadow ran towards him bearing its little fangs.

A very startled Nuno leapt straight into the air and onto the top of a container. He was certainly safe there, but he was so embarrassed that he was glad no one else was there to see this shame. As shame boiled into anger, he pulled himself together and leapt down onto the bouncing hysterical rat threatening him below. It was over in a second. But before Nuno could enjoy his meal, four more rats ran out of the shadows and attacked him!

Nuno's first impulse was to escape like before. He simply was not used to prey fighting back instead of fleeing. But at that moment his heart turned back into that of the natural hunter killer he was born to be.

Nuno was surrounded by four rats threatening to spring on him at any second. He whispered to himself between growls, "I'm at least ten times bigger. Have to admit they are brave little fools."

Then, he reached out and caught one in his claws, ripping it open. He grabbed another in his jaws and with a jerk of his mouth, broke it. The other two started to run. Nuno pounced on another, dispatching it at once. The remaining one ran as fast as anything Nuno ever saw in the fields. But he was determined not to let it get away.

As the rat twisted and turned around the scattered containers, Nuno's sharp night eyes kept it in sight. The little thing was slowing down as it had grown fat on the ship. Nuno started pouncing but always missed as it managed to stay just one second ahead. Quickly, it disappeared through a grated space in the wall. Nuno could squeeze through it, but he remembered he already had four meals waiting for him back where it all started, and his stomach was ready for its midnight snack.

Taking note of the grated wall, he returned and carried all four rats to a safe space between two containers. He ate two of them because one just did not seem to be enough. He decided they were foul, too, but not as bad as pigeon. Neither his stomach nor his intestines complained later.

Normally, he would never kill more than he could eat. Lynxes always thought there was something immoral about that. But this

was self-defense. Lynxes never had anything against that. Nuno's instinct would not let him leave his other two kills in case another lynx would find them and steal them. Of course, there were no other lynxes there. But just in case, Nuno decided to stay in his little space with a paw resting on top of his next meal and take a long nap.

He did not notice when the moonlight gave way to sunlight as the new day lit up the lower deck from openings above. Suddenly, ghastly demon shrieks poured down from the sky, making him jump in panic. He was ready to defend his little space with back arched, fur on end, and his little stubby tail twitching. Had the rat gods returned for vengeance?

Then the sunlight was blocked by a container being lowered into the hold by a screeching crane. The container dropped onto another one that was just within sight from his hiding place. There was a man with a ladder who climbed up and detached the chains holding the container. The crane lifted the chains out of the hold, turned to the dock where it would haul another container on to the ship. The man with the ladder filled Nuno's heart with dread. This was the only other animal on the entire Iberian Peninsula that was a direct threat to Nuno and all his kind.

As far as Nuno could understand from all the stories and his own limited experience, people were not really bad, just incredibly careless. They did not hunt lynxes to kill them for fun or meat. But it was their traps meant for others, their cars on night roads, and worst of all, destroying the overgrown fields and forests where lynxes and their cherished rabbits lived. The rabbits had the worst of it. They were hunted for their meat. But as the rabbits dwindled in number, so did the lynxes. No one could think of loving and reproducing when their empty stomachs growled and ached for days on end. This is what drove Nuno from his friends and family to California.

Regardless, they were to be avoided at all cost. They were ten times bigger than Nuno, but the fact that they needed ladders to climb just to the top of one container, while Nuno could easily with one leap jump to the top of two, meant that he should not be too worried. But he still decided to stay out of sight. They seemed to only come down to the hold during the day.

By the end of the day, Nuno got used to the screeching cranes and the moving containers. As the sunlight was drifting away, the few men in the hold left and the cranes stopped. Nuno felt calm enough to eat his last two rats.

As the moon rose in the sky, Nuno's natural curiosity grew. He wanted to explore more of the ship, especially that strange, inviting, grilled space in the wall where the last rat had fled to safety.

CHAPTER THREE

As Nuno returned to the curious grill, a great vibration passed through the whole ship that sent him scurrying back to hide. The ship was coming alive with noises and lights as its mighty engines growled to life. The ropes were pulled up, and many shouts filled the air. The ship slowly drifted to the center of the river and then with great power and decisiveness the two engines propelled it toward the open sea to the west.

Nuno would learn the ship's schedule very soon. The sailors returned to their normal four-hour shifts and patrolled on the deck above. Fortunately, no one cared to enter the hold Nuno shared with his strange rat foes.

The ship passed the little lighthouse on the small island where the Tejo River met the Atlantic Ocean. It passed the Casino town of Estoril with its ex-royalty, then with the Cascais lighthouse in the distance, the ship turned south and headed to Africa. It was a bit over two hours before Nuno was calm enough to try exploring again.

Nuno approached the grill carefully with intense sniffing. A flow of nasty smelling air was being sucked in. He overcame his whiskers' warning of the tight fit and squeezed through. In the distance he could make out fan blades slowly spinning. His keen eyes cut through the gloom.

After the large fan, the metal tunnel separated in many directions. With good timing, he could pass the fan blades on the first try. If not, his backside would get a good smacking. He decided to follow the tunnel that smelled better than the others. This strategy led him to the mess hall and kitchen. He stared through the grate, considering his next move. The green glow of the emergency exit light revealed a good ship-shape kitchen, but the mess hall had leftovers on the tables and open cans of more uneaten food.

Though the kitchen had limited hours for cooking, the mess hall was always open for sailors to have meals and snacks throughout the day and night. On one of the tables, he saw one of those rats, maybe the same one who escaped him the night before. He had to stifle a growl so as not to warn the little runt.

Slowly and quietly, Nuno squeezed through the grate and moved to the shadows. He slowly moved to the edge of the table, crouched back, and pounced on the unsuspecting rat. Nuno's force carried him and the rat across the table and onto the floor with empty soda cans clanging all around them. This so startled them both that they froze behind a counter where Nuno's pounce brought them.

Suddenly, a door opened, and the lights flashed on. Nuno pulled himself behind the counter and held his breath. The rat's little heart pounded between his paws.

Hearing the crash, the sailor yelled out in the excitable Tagalog of his native Philippines. Calmed down somewhat, he entered the kitchen, opened the refrigerator. and took out a sandwich and another can of soda. He put the sandwich in the microwave and heated it up. Then he took both to a clear space on one of the mess tables. The kitchen crew would clean everything up before breakfast.

He was taking his time eating his warm sandwich and reading a colorful comic book. Neither Nuno nor the rat dared to make a move. After hyperventilating for a while, the rat calmed down and whispered to Nuno.

"We come from the same place near Xisto. I also wanted to

escape that poor region and try my luck in this strange California."

"How can you speak my language?"

"I've always been good at picking up foreign languages. It's my hobby. I can also speak rabbit and hare."

"What a smart rodent you are. Too bad you are still a rodent and I will eat you after this sailor leaves."

"Now, you see, I was just getting to that. You may have noticed that at night this place is a mess. There is enough for us both to share and eat. I could be an important ally. I have been here longer than you and know the entire ship. I can show you all the secret places. I have even picked up much of the people language. Basically, what I am saying is that I can be of great help to you. We can look out for one another. You never know when one of these sailors will pop up behind you."

"What did that person just say?" Nuno tested the rat.

"He said, 'What's that noise? Who's in here? No one? Well, I might as well get something to eat while I am here' or something like that."

As Nuno considered the rat's plea, the sailor rose and threw his half-eaten sandwich and soda into an open trash can, then left. Luckily for the vagabonds, this was often the fate of free food. As the lights were turned off, the room came under the green gloom again, returning the two to their conversation. Nuno's mouth started to water, and a few drops fell on the rat's face.

The rat quickly continued, "N-N-Now as I w-w-was s-s-saying, we could help each other. There's still a long trip ahead of us. I have done this trip over a dozen times and I can teach you how to make it smooth and even enjoyable. O-o-o-of course, you could eat me now, b-b-but I would only be one meal for one day. Then you would be alone to face the unknown. Besides, I can show you that there is more than enough food without eating me. Wh-Wh-What d-d-do you s-s-say?"

Nuno had to consider that. He was not used to making quick decisions. In fact, the only real decision he made in his whole life was making the strange journey to California. Everything he did was ruled by instinct and every instinct in his mind was telling him to eat the pathetic rodent tightly held in his paws. But then again, a hometown rat that spoke his language was too bizarre for words.

Should he accept the rat's offer of being allies (being friends was too much of a stretch)? Nuno could always eat him later, though something did not seem right about that in his mind. No, he had to decide now. As he thought, the smell of the half-eaten chicken sandwich entered his awareness.

As he sniffed, the rat blurted out, "And I w-w-will always g-g-give you first choice in any food we find, like that sandwich we both can smell."

Nuno finally spoke, "Fine, let's try it. You understand that this goes against everything we lynxes believe in, but I admit I am a bit out of my comfort zone. If you don't hold your side of this bargain, I will hunt you down and play with you until you have a heart attack and die in my paws. Another thing, don't you ever tell another lynx that Nuno made friends with a rodent. Do you understand?"

"Oh, yes, I understand. Anything you say." Came the murmured reply.

"I can't hear you, talking rodent!"

"Yes, yes, YES, fine. ANYTHING YOU SAY!" He squeaked as loud as he could, sounding like an old wooden door creaking open.

"Fine. Now what?"

"Well, first thing is I suggest you finish that sailor's sandwich."

"Don't mind if I do. Do you rodents have names?" Nuno released him and approached the trash can.

"Yes. Mine is Papa Figo, but you can call me Figo for short. I was born under a fig tree and my mother noticed how much I loved eating the figs that fell on the ground and…"

"Got it. More information than I need, Figo." Nuno snapped. "Like I told you earlier, my name is…."

"Yes, I remember, Nuno."

"Another rule: only I can interrupt the other one. Got it?"

"Whatever you say, sir."

Nuno approached the trash can and fished the sandwich out. Placing one paw on the sandwich, he tore large pieces from it with his mouth. He looked over at the still nervous shuddering Figo and said, "Not bad, but I still wonder if a rodent sandwich wouldn't be better." But in reality, Nuno enjoyed a meal with no bones and fur to deal with. He ate the whole thing, but the salt in the sandwich made Nuno very thirsty.

"Water, ratty Figo, water! Where can we find that?"

"Follow me." Figo led Nuno into the kitchen and climbed up to the sink with the leaking faucet.

"You have already proven you have some worth." Nuno could smell the water and followed Figo into the sink where he could drink from the small puddle formed below the spigot. Figo leapt as fast as he could out and away from the big thirsty wild cat.

Back on the floor, Nuno started a habit to always identify a quick escape route wherever he was. Doors could suddenly open and if he was trapped, no way of knowing what those mariners would do to him. Nuno would desperately fight with tooth and claw, but people have the strange ability to grab and hold things, making any nearby thing a weapon. No, best to flee. They were within a few bounds of the wall grate where they entered not too long ago.

"All right, Figo, now what? Seems we have the food and water questions solved."

"When you feel like you have to pass some scat, make sure you do that among the containers somewhere hard to find. If these sailors were to find it, they would certainly start a thorough search."

"Got it."

"As for me, I haven't eaten yet. I'll take a look in that trash can for something. You can do whatever you want."

"I'll wait here by the grate. Go get something to eat."

Figo jumped into the trash can, burrowed through its contents, and found something. Suddenly the door opened, and the lights came on. Nuno squeezed behind the grate and looked out. Another sailor grabbed a small bag from the cabinet. As he walked to the microwave, his foot knocked the trash can a bit, causing some serious movement inside.

He placed the bag inside the microwave and turned it on. Much to Nuno's fascination, the bag soon produced furious popping sounds. It died down, and the sailor left with the strange bag, now much enlarged. Nuno could not imagine what kind of animal was inside. Figo leapt out and ran to join Nuno behind the grate.

"Did you eat enough?" Nuno asked.

"No, but I think I'll be fine until tomorrow. That knock nearly gave me a heart attack!"

"I've had enough adventures for one night. Time for sleep."

"May I suggest we sleep inside these air tunnels?"

"But it smells bad here."

"Yes, but follow me. I'll show you a tunnel where it doesn't smell bad."

Nuno followed Figo to a section of the air ducts that separated from the smelly one from the hold. He agreed that it was better than sleeping with the containers. They laid down together with Nuno wrapping his paw around Figo like he would a kitten lynx. It took Figo hours to feel comfortable, but soon sleep overwhelmed his fear. The end of the next day, they would reach Casablanca.

CHAPTER FOUR

Being both nocturnal animals, they at least shared the same sleep patterns. They awoke at the same time, as the sun was almost concluding its descent toward the ocean and the ship was approaching Casablanca harbor. Just as Nuno was thinking of breakfast, the entire city erupted in a great moan. Nuno fled into a corner of the air tunnel, shaking in fear. Had the city been taken over by demons?

Figo laughed, "Oh come on! Have you never heard the Muslim call to prayer? The sun is almost set, and that is one of the times when all the mosques call out 'Allahu Akbar!' with their loudspeakers. The next time will be just as the sun starts to rise. It will be close to the time we would be going to sleep."

"Oh, yes, I knew that. Guess I was still not awake yet," Nuno sputtered, hiding his ignorance of such a simple fact. "So, what does 'Allahu Akbar' mean, anyway?"

"Beats me," Figo shrugged. "I don't even know what 'prayer' means, either. But that's how one of the local rat folks explained it to me the first time I was here. At the smaller ports like this one, the ship only has a few containers to load or unload. We should be underway to the next port of Dakar, Senegal after noon tomorrow."

The dock workers secured the ship to the wharf.

"Do you hear that?" Figo asked. "That's traditional Moroccan music playing from the dock's loudspeakers."

Nuno listened to the very rhythmic music with its soulful almost mournful singing. An hour later the ship was secure. The music and the lights abruptly were turned off, except for the few ship lights that kept the top deck awash in a pale light only as bright as a full moon.

Nuno asked Figo, "Now, what?"

"Now, we go into town and find some real food, Moroccan food."

"Leave the ship? What if the ship leaves without us?"

"The ship is going nowhere. Many of the sailors will go into town for a good meal and some fun, too. Besides, even if the ship does leave without us, why would we worry? We'll just wait a few weeks for the next one."

Nuno was completely baffled by the incredibly easy-going Figo. Of course, it helped to be knowledgeable about the journey. It also helped to be small enough to fit through a drainage hole. At nine kilograms, Nuno was limited in the holes he could escape through. He also had been raised to be fearful of everything. He had to overcome a lot to agree to follow the rat down the securing ropes to the wharf.

There were round disks attached to the ropes to keep rats from climbing onboard, but Figo had a run-and-jump technique that let him cross these barriers. Nuno could just step over them. Apparently, no one thought to keep lynxes out.

They hid behind the shadows of a crane. The port was empty of people and motion. The moon was high in the sky but provided little light, being a mere quarter of itself.

"Let's go this way. I know a great couscous restaurant nearby. But you must promise me something, Nuno. You absolutely cannot attack rats anymore. We'll probably meet some of my friends here. If you play nice, they will show us many interesting things. Can you promise me this?"

"It runs against everything I know, Figo. For example, it's incredibly difficult for me to not eat you right now. But you are proving useful in many strange ways." Nuno liked playing with Figo's mind, though he had already accepted their strange arrangement. Figo got to live and Nuno was taught everything about how to make this strange trip not so stressful. Seemed fair to him.

"Then you better stay here, or I will wake up the big guard dog they have here." Figo's voice tried to not quiver so much.

"Oh, come on, Figo. I was only joking. I never tried it, but couscous sounds better than raw rat. What did you say about a guard dog? Big, did you say? Just how big?"

"If you're a good kitty, you will never have the pleasure to meet Ahmad. He's not particularly big as dogs go, but still five times bigger than you. He's not very smart, has a rather violent nature. Seems to not like cats very much."

"Hey, bozo, I am not a cat! I'm a lynx."

"Try explaining the difference to him. Hope your Arabic is in good form."

"Oh, never mind. Let's try this couscous you talk about. As for you, smarty pants, I am sure we can find some local cats who would enjoy meeting you and your friends."

"I doubt that. Moroccan cats don't like lynxes. Have you smelled yourself lately? They would run away in disgust."

"Now, I know you're joking. We've only met a few nights ago. How do you know what I normally smell like? Enough of this silliness. Let's just keep an eye out for each other. I'm getting really hungry. Let's go."

"Fine. See that drainage pipe coming through that embankment over there? Let's run to it but stay in the shadows."

They both ran to the pipe that was dripping rainwater slowly into a drain that fed directly into the bay. They rain through the dark pipe with Nuno complaining under his breath about wet paws. Out the other side was a small stream that disappeared into the darkness ahead.

"Good, now see that light over there? That's the restaurant and bar, built for sailors. We will avoid the front and go down that dark alley next to it to the back where they throw away the leftovers of the meals the sailors didn't finish. Got it?"

"Yes, I understand your Xisto Portuguese fine." And Nuno started for the dark alley.

There was only a small light over the back door. The big trash bins were against a fence to the side of the door with their lids open. Loud Moroccan pop music came from the restaurant.

"Wait here," Figo whispered. "I will check out the situation and motion for you to come when the coast is clear."

He ran along the wall and hid in the shadow by the trash cans. Nuno could see a few other small shadows gathered around. They seemed pleased to meet him. Suddenly, they all scampered up the rain pipe and into the full trash bins, disappearing within the trash.

Hey, thought Nuno, he forgot about me! Nuno crept along the shadowy wall slowly. Suddenly, he saw four larger shadows leap to the top of the trash heap and started to paw at the trash. They were looking for something in particular. They were looking for rats!

"Cats!" yelled Figo's familiar voice. "Nuno!"

Nuno leapt the short distance to the trash pile with claws stretched.

"الوشق!" [alwshq! Lynx!] cried one of the cats and the four shadows fled in four directions. But the smaller rat shadows also disappeared into four different directions.

"No! Come back! This is my friend, Nuno. He is your friend, too!" Figo squeaked to the disappearing shadows. But none of the shadows came back.

Figo looked at the rat tail he was holding in his hand and began to cry hysterically, "My tail! I lost my tail!"

"That's someone else's tail. Yours is still attached to your backside, silly." Nuno calmed him.

Having survived all that excitement, Figo sighed, "Looks like we have to feast on lamb and chicken couscous by ourselves."

"What are these soft things in the couscous?" Nuno asked. "They have no taste at all."

"You mean these? They're dates and golden raisins. You can't taste them? Oh, that's right. Cat folk can't taste anything sweet.

"How many times do I have to tell you? I am not a cat."

"Whatever, but you have the taste buds of cats. Anyway, this is my favorite part of the trip, to taste the different cuisines at the various ports we will land at. For example, here they like to use cinnamon with their meat. If I had opposable thumbs, I would carry a bag with me and flavor all the meat I find with it."

"Yes, I agree, little friend. But I also like the different music. We lynxes have soul. That's something you rodent folk don't have."

"Will you stop calling me a rodent! Sounds like a field mouse. You can certainly tell the difference, I hope."

"Look, I'll stop calling you a rodent when you start growing fur on your tail."

"Well, then I will continue calling you……"

"No, you won't. You will call me Sir Nuno, a prince of the Lynx tribe. Got it?"

"Whatever, Sir Nuno. Let's explore a little before returning to the ship."

"Don't you think we've seen enough?"

"Now who is the scaredy cat—I mean, scaredy lynx?"

Nuno grabbed Figo with his front paw, letting his claws sink just a bit, and brought him up to eye level. "There are no scaredy lynxes here! As far as I can see, there is just one scared rodent shaking in my paw. Don't you agree?"

"Fine, fine, whatever you say! There is just a scared rodent here. A scared rodent. A scared…. Just put me down!"

Nuno put him down. Figo asked himself, what did I do to deserve this?

Nuno gave himself a good shake of his body like he was shaking off any unpleasantries that had recently attached to him. "Yes, I agree we should explore a bit. Seems like you have been here many times. What else can you show me? Though I do have a strong curiosity streak, I would prefer that we stay in sight of the ship."

"Fine. Now, let's see. I know! There is a grove of fruit trees nearby. I like a nice piece of fruit after a big meal. How about that?"

"No! I have no interest in fruit. I only eat meat and sometimes the little bits that are attached, like couscous. You apparently like to eat anything and everything."

"In fact, I do. You so limit yourself by only eating meat. Do you mean to say you have never tried our wonderful Portuguese Pastéis de Nata with cinnamon on top (egg tarts)? Oh, I forgot, nothing sweet. And yet, our homeland is famous for its sweets."

"Yes, nothing sweet, but I do eat milk products like cheese, cream, even ice cream. Just nothing made of chocolate."

"But there's nothing better than a homemade chocolate fudge pie. I remember waiting eagerly outside the house of an old woman near where I was born. She made the best. My mother, rest her soul, turned me on to it."

"Funny, that was the one thing my mother told me to never eat. Apparently, it does nasty things to our innards."

"All right just forget about it. I'll show you something else. Follow me." Figo led Nuno across the road and back through the water drainage pipe. Then, he turned left, and they ran over rocks and rubble, as they kept the sea to their right. They covered a kilometer in about thirty minutes, with Nuno having to wait several times for Figo.

They stopped in the shadow of a huge mosque perched by the sea. "What is it, Figo?"

"That, my friend, is the Hassan II Mosque. My local friends tell me it's the largest mosque in Africa."

"Now, Figo, don't make me growl. What is a mosque?"

"Well, it's that. That's a mosque."

"Anything else you want to tell me?" Nuno asked with a slight growl.

"Let's see. It's a place where many people come at certain times of the day and go down on their knees all facing the same direction, east, I believe. It's also the place that makes those loud mournful noises you heard when we entered the port. That is how people know when to go to the mosque."

"But why do they do that?"

"I don't know. My local friends use the word 'prayer' but none of us knows what that means."

"People are so mysterious. Would love to learn more about them, but we just can't trust them. They would throw me in a gawking prison and you, well, they'd simply kill you."

"Yes, you're right. I even must be careful of what I eat and you, too, by the way. People put out poison to kill me and my brothers, but any hungry animal will eat it and die, including lynxes."

"Even where we come from, this is true. I had a cousin who ate it, and he died a long agonizing death as his insides were slowly melted into jelly. Well, that's how he described it. He just made it back to our village, but there was nothing we could do. That reminds me we should really hate these people. But somehow I can't get past my curiosity."

"Didn't realize you were so sensitive, Nuno. My curiosity doesn't extend so far."

They were interrupted by the loud call to prayer coming from the tall minaret.

"Nuno! Where did the night go? Hurry! We have to make it to the ship before they start working."

So, the two unlikely friends hurried back to the ship and to their little lair in the air shaft. There they quickly fell asleep. This time Figo did not mind the heavy paw wrapped around him. He remembered how Nuno saved him and his friends from the cats. Instead of a threat, the paw was becoming more of a security blanket.

CHAPTER FIVE

After three days at sea, they approached Dakar, Senegal. It only took one day from Lisboa to Casablanca. Nuno was already edgy. He was tired of sneaking into the kitchen at night and eating from the trash cans. He yearned to when he could catch his dinner the honest way, stalking and pouncing. Not rooting through rubbish like a beggar.

"Hey, Figo, what's with this humid air? My skin is itching from it." Nuno set to rigorously scratching below his left ear with his back paw.

"You better stop complaining about something you have no control over. As my dear old Pa used to say, 'If you can change something you don't like, then change it. If you can't change it, then accept it.' Besides, we have an even longer trip after this. The next leg of our journey to Recife in Brazil will be one day longer."

"Fine, oh wise one. What is the plan to get off this rusty can and breathe some fresh air?"

"Won't know until I can ask some of my local buddies. How's your French?"

"Are you joking? I can barely speak Portuguese. I didn't have many years of schooling like you obviously did. How long do rodents live, anyway?"

"We live long enough to learn all the important things in life. Life is not all about rabbits and football (soccer in the US)."

"Careful, little friend. Careful, my VERY little friend."

"Little friend says let's go to the container hold and see where the sun is."

The odd couple ventured to the familiar stale oily hold with the maze of containers stacked like children's wooden blocks. The sun had already ushered in the dusk.

"I think we can go for a little walk. At dusk, all cats are grey. No, no, I mean all lynxes are grey. And all rodents, too. See, we are practically grey even as I speak."

"I'll let you talk your way out of that one only because I'm in a good mood. I'll soon satisfy my curiosity of a new place. Stop mouthing off and show us the way."

Nuno followed Figo down the rope securing the ship to the wharf. They scampered to the darker shadows of one of the loading cranes.

"Hey, Figo. I smell a different vermin stink over there in the bushes. Must be a few of your local buddies. Go find out what's going on tonight. I am ready for some adventure."

"I'll go check it out. You stay here. No need to frighten my friends to death." With that he ran and disappeared into the bushes.

After waiting for a while, Nuno was becoming both bored and worried, the worst combination. He wondered if he should find out what was going on and go over to the bushes. He realized that he had come to rely on Figo and perhaps he should be a bit nicer to him. Just as he was contemplating such an absurdity, he saw Figo come out of the bushes and motioned for him to come over.

"Come here, Nuno. I want to introduce you to a little friend of mine. Nadine, this is Nuno. Nuno, this.... Hey, where are you running off to? Come back! He's a friend!"

"Should I bring it back? It'll be in my mouth, that's the only way I can carry anything."

"No, no, that's fine. It's a she, by the way. We are, ah... friends from the several trips I have taken here. We were ah.... making up for lost time. I mean, you know, catching up on the family news. Family, I mean what a family! It grows every year. In fact, some of her family is mine, too. But we rat men are not always there for our children. I mean, I only met my dear old Pa when he came to visit Ma. Well, and I don't know how else to explain it. I mean I...."

"Figo! You can stop now. You're not making any sense at all. So, what did she say about what's going on now? Did she say anything about any nice pretty lynxettes around here?"

"What's a lynxette? No! She said nothing about lynxes of any kind. However, later tonight there is a Mbalax party at one of the empty warehouses nearby. You like music, right?"

"Indeed, I do! That would be really cool! Yeah, let's go!"

"First, we must find something to eat. They have great food here. It's way too early for parties now. There is a simple port dive bar and restaurant on the way. Let's go."

Figo trotted off to the dim lights in the near distance. Nuno followed Figo and the very enticing spicy scent coming from the small lonely mud-colored box by the side of the empty port road.

As usual, they crept to the back and quickly found the trash bins full of half-eaten meals. The stale smell of beer bottles came from another bin off to the side. They leapt on top of the barely closed plastic bags and easily tore into them.

"What's this I'm tasting, connoisseur of all things wonderful? This is delicious."

"What makes the food of West Africa so special are the spices and the ground nuts they use for the sauces. Peanuts are quite common. And yes, I know peanuts are not a nut. What can I do? I didn't make the word up. I just eat it whenever I can."

"I especially like the lamb and the fish versions. Hey, what's that?"

"Dive down to the bottom!"

Just then, someone from the restaurant with another handful of empty beer bottles and a plastic bag of new rubbish noisily approached the trash cans. As he threw the bag onto the pile, he noticed a lot of movement of the bags below.

"Rats maudits!" [Damn rats!]

He grabbed a nearby broom stick and started slamming it into the dark bottom of the trash bin, hoping to break a rat's body. What he did do was pinch the tail of a much larger denizen of the darkness. The owner of said tail leapt out of the trash bin with a great growl towards the broomstick assailant, who ran screaming back into the restaurant.

By the time he returned with a shotgun and fired into the trash can, our two heroes had already escaped into the bushes. The shotgun blast made them run across the dark empty lot and into an abandoned building. The restaurant manager and a few other waiters tackled the hysterical man to the ground where they held him.

He was screaming from the top of his lungs, "Un démon, un démon, je dis. Un démon dans la corbeille m'a attaqué!" [A demon, a demon, I say. A demon in the trash bin attacked me!]

The restaurant patrons surrounded them. This was the most excitement they had since Youssou pulled a knife on Titi for flirting with his man, Fatou a few months before. That set off a bar fight with people being thrown through windows and chairs smashing tables. Luckily, no one got hurt seriously.

Panting heavily, our two friends hid in the darkest corner they could find. Once they caught their breath, Nuno spoke. "Figo, we cannot do that again!"

"But Nuno, that is where the food is. Do you think we can just walk into the restaurant, sit at a table, and order off the menu?"

"Ah, you're right. Maybe we go later in the night?"

"These sailor dive bars stay open all night. Besides, the food is better when it's still warm. It's the price we pay for eating in the world of humans."

"But why are they so violent against us?"

"Oh, my friend, it's not us they hate. It's me and all my rodent friends. Under normal circumstances they would probably like you and make you stay with them, treating you as a member of the family. As for me, they want to exterminate us and that is the word they use."

"But why? You're very harmless, even pathetically so."

"How would I know? I just eat the things they don't want anymore. What's the harm in that?"

"Let me get this straight, they are afraid of a harmless rodent, but not me who could rip their hand off?"

"Yes, you could say it that way."

"Wow, they are either stupid or crazy."

"My experience is they are both and to be kept far away."

"Then, why do you choose a life that is so close to them? When I get to California, I hope to never see another one again."

"I guess I like the change of scenery. I guess it beats a life of hawks and lynxes always stalking us. Did I say lynxes? Sorry, I meant snakes."

"I know what you meant. You're right. You know, I wouldn't mind eating a hawk or even a snake right now."

"Nuno, you're all right. You really are. I think it's time to hear some wild music to take our minds off our respective positions on the Value Chain of Life. Let's go."

Staying in the shadows, they approached an old derelict warehouse. They could hear heavy percussion with very danceable music full of joy and possibility coming through the broken windows. But how to get in? Figo led them around to the back away from the one door that opened and had a line of young people that went around the corner twenty meters long.

There, just above a stack of old wooden pallets, was a dark window with no glass left. Figo led the way. He climbed up the pallets and stopped on the windowsill. Nuno followed with one leap. They leapt down onto piles of old coiled rope. There were just a few rays of moonlight leaking through the broken windows and a hole in the roof. But it was enough for their sharp eyes.

They ran up rotting stairs high up to an equally rotting wooden door that blocked their path to the roof.

"Now, what?" Figo asked disappointedly.

"Now, what? We go to the roof and listen to some great music. I feel like dancing already." Nuno leapt with his two front paws and pushed the door off its hinges.

They crept over to the edge of the roof that looked down into the large open space below that made for an impromptu dance floor with a DJ and his equipment just below them. People were enthusiastically dancing to the wonderful music called Mbalax. They hovered just above the dancers and no one noticed two shadows looking down from above, one with exceptionally long hairy ears. After a while, Nuno could not help himself and started to dance himself, moving in a way that only lynxes can.

Suddenly, the edge of the roof collapsed, and the two music lovers fell down into the crowd. There were screams and a rush to the door when the large furry shadow of Nuno fell right in front of the DJ, who jumped on top of his speakers, but left the music playing. Nuno ran and leapt outside through an open window. All eyes were on Nuno. No one noticed a much smaller shadow moving along the side of the wall toward the door, being too small to leap so high as Nuno could.

As soon as Nuno was outside, he realized Figo could not follow him. Figo had to go out the door, but he would certainly be stepped on by a hundred feet. Nuno ran to the doorway and immediately those hundred feet ran back into the warehouse, allowing little Figo to run out. Together they ran all the way back to the ship.

Safely in their cozy air shaft, their hearts slowly calmed, and they could breathe normally.

"That was too much adventure, Figo! We nearly were killed twice in one night. Remind me to stay on the ship until we get to California."

"I hear you, Nuno. But in three days' time, we will be ready to try our luck in Brazil. You know they speak Portuguese there. Well, a kind of Portuguese."

"I don't intend to get into any conversation there, except with my

favorite rodent. Now, it's time for some sleep."

Figo smiled and quickly fell asleep between his two favorite lynx paws.

CHAPTER SIX

The trip across the Atlantic to Recife, Brazil went smoothly enough except one night Nuno tipped over the trash can in the dining room, waking up the cook sleeping in the next room. Besides making a great mess on the floor, it also caused a general rat hunt the next day. But our two heroes missed all that fuss by sleeping the day away safely snug in their hidden lair in the air duct.

The ship tied up at port midmorning. Around 1400, the cranes creaked to work and started the process of removing and replacing containers in the hold. The banging of heavy containers and the screeching of old gears ended the possibility of any more sleep. They snuck out of their hideout and watched all the commotion from the shadows. Music was being badly distorted from the old speakers.

"Ah, the music," Figo sighed. "This is my favorite. I guess old Tiago is the Port Master today. When young Miguel is in charge, he plays that Carioca Funk. But this, my friend, is Forró. Now, this is music. Forró bands usually have three or four accordions and they are coming through fine now. This really gets the Brazilian she-rats in the mood."

"Don't know, Figo. I don't think I like it very much. We clearly have different music tastes. I would not want to go to any Forró parties tonight. Would not be worth the adventure. That Senegalese music, however. That was worth the fright the roof gave us."

"Don't tell me you prefer that Bosso Novo stuff? I mean they play Garota de Ipanema even in hotel lobbies in China."

"China? Where is that? And yes, I do like Bosso Nova. We can hear it even in Xisto in the evenings from the open windows of the old slate farmhouses."

"Oh, never mind. We're not going there this trip. But if you ever want a real adventure, tell me and I will take you to Shanghai."

"I can tell you now, this is my last adventure, and it will end in California."

"No worries. You'll get bored soon enough. Everyone's bored there. And when that happens to you, let me know. There is a big world out there."

"So far, all I can say is that all the ports look the same. Not interesting at all."

"Of course, but if you dare to watch your ship disappear into the horizon and stay behind to really explore your new home, then you can see many real interesting things."

"Fine but remember that you can immediately fit in with the millions of rodent folks who live in these port cities. But what about me? I can't live in cities. Just not possible."

They were in the middle of discussing this interesting point when all the noise suddenly stopped as the sun was lowering in the sky. The darkening silence caused them to be silent, too. They waited in their corner until dusk really settled in, ushering in the darkness of night.

"Time to eat black beans with rice and find some Brazilian action." Figo was the first to break the silence.

"I think you are on your own tonight, Figo. I have no idea what beans and rice are, but I am sure I have no interest. I'll look for some grilled fish and listen to the lapping ocean for a change."

"You want to do what? Oh no, no, you can't miss a night on the town in Brazil. You simply must come with me. I have many friends here."

"I doubt I would be interested in a 'night on the town.' I don't even know what that means. I am just a simple country lynx that doesn't understand cities."

"Suit yourself, old lynx. I'm out of here." And Figo ran up and out of the ship.

"Figo! Wait! The ship is loaded and ready to go. How do you know it won't leave early, like tonight?"

Figo stopped in his tracks. "Oh, damn it, Nuno. You know, you're right. Sometimes you actually do make sense. Dammit again. Oh, all right. Let's find something grilled and we'll watch the moon cross the sky, listening to the water at our feet. Boring! If it weren't for you, I'd have half a mind to let the ship go and stay here until it comes again. But what would I do with you for a month?"

"Oh, don't worry, little rodent. You don't have to worry about me. I will definitely be on this ship when it leaves, either tonight or tomorrow morning."

"But then who would keep you out of trouble on the rest of the voyage? Guess, you're stuck with me tonight, again."

"Again."

"Luckily, the city starts just outside the port gates. There is a good selection of seaside restaurants not too far. Let's go."

Just as the sun lowered behind the city, our two friends crept out of the ship and through a hole in the port fence to the outside. Their ship was the closest to the front gate and within ten minutes of leaving they were behind a row of restaurants with trash bins already half full. The patrons sat on small wharves and docks over the water. So, the trash bins were off to the sides and out of the way.

They snuck below the wooden planks under the busy tables that formed the floor. Sometimes a wave would roll under the dock, causing Figo to leap onto the back of Nuno to avoid drowning. Nuno did not mind, as the humid air made his back itchy and Figo's little paws provided some relief. Figo liked it up there, making him feel safe from the threats of the universe.

They found a secluded group of trash bins with lids opened. They dove right in and started eating. Nuno found quite a few half-eaten grilled fish with their heads intact. Figo found a favorite Brazilian traditional dish, black beans and rice.

"Must be Wednesday, whatever that means. It's the day of rice and beans. Try some, Nuno."

Nuno sniffed and shook his head, "Are you crazy? Why would you eat that instead of this wonderful fish? By the way, you know I am only a flesh-eater."

"Don't worry. I'll get to the fish later." Of course, Figo could only eat one bean and three bits of rice before he was full. He only had room for a small morsel of fish. Nuno could eat four half-eaten fish.

After their meal, which would last them a whole day, they jumped out and looked for a nice place to watch the ocean at night. There was such a place close to the port fence which obligingly had rocks to hide behind.

"You know, Figo, there really isn't anything like watching the sea at night under the broad moonlight. I never had a chance back home. We lived too far away."

"Yes, you're right. I've seen it so many times, I don't even notice its charms anymore."

"No? How could you not? Don't you see how the moon light shimmers on the water? As the water moves, the light sparkles and shines. The sound of the waves brings such peace to the soul. The cool sea breeze caresses our faces. It brings comfort and joy."

"Well, that it does, Nuno. I believe you could be a poet, if you could write. But no matter. You can still be a bard, telling wonderful poetic stories to everyone resting after dinner by the sea or around a campfire."

"Not sure I understand all that, but it sounds good."

After some time of pause and reflection, Figo asked, "Nuno, do you believe we have souls?"

"What do you think a soul is?"

"A soul contains the essence of who we are and lives forever,

even after our bodies die."

"It lives forever? But where does it go after our bodies are gone?"

"Now, that is the ultimate question, Nuno. We rat folk have been asking that question since the beginning. Some say there is a place up in the sky like a huge ripe grain field where our souls go that has everything we need for a blissful afterlife. And the bad ones go to a terrible place of salt and fire. Perhaps it was a salty fire. Don't remember.

"Others say, our souls stay here and float about living in trees or wherever suits us, being invisible to everyone still alive. We'll have no physical needs nor even minds to get bored. Some even say that we have no souls and we only have the few years of life, then nothing."

"Nothing? Hmm, don't like the sound of that. What is a bad one?"

"Never could understand what a 'bad one' means. People seem to think we are bad ones. That's why they are always trying to kill us. But what are we doing that angers them so? So, we eat the things they throw away. Is that a crime?"

"Maybe it's because you have fleas?"

"That's ridiculous! We have fleas, you have fleas, they have fleas. So what? How do they know that it's not their fleas getting on us? That's no excuse for all the traps and poison. Besides, is it a crime to have fleas?"

"Don't know, either. Never could understand them. Some shoot us and others try to protect us. Others simply hit us with their cars without a thought one way or the other."

"What does it mean to be a bad lynx or a good one? A bad rat or a good one? We never make moral choices. We just do our thing, whatever pops into our heads. And whatever pops into our heads is quite simple and narrow in scope. We are either finding something to eat, a mate to love, or somewhere safe to sleep. That's it." Figo continued.

"Maybe it's the eating part they don't like. I mean we eat rabbits; they eat rabbits. They eat grain; you eat grain."

"Oh, give me a break. The amount of grain they grow compared to what we eat is much more. Judging from how much bread or uneaten rice I see in the trash bins of the world; we clearly have no impact on the availability of grain-made food. Have you ever been in a supermarket at night?"

"I'm not really sure what a supermarket is but go on."

"It's a huge building full of all the things people eat. They don't have to eat rabbits. They have a dozen other kinds of meat to choose from. Grains? Every type you can imagine and many you can't. No, it has to be something else."

"I don't know. All I know is we can't trust them and should avoid them at all costs."

"We can agree on that!"

They sat in silence pondering the weighty conversation they just had and wherever their thoughts would wander from that. Meanwhile, the moon moved slowly across the sky and the rhythm of the waves lulled them almost to sleep.

Suddenly, a loud foghorn burst through the night sky. Their ship! The lights were all on and was full of activity.

"Nuno! Our ship! It's leaving! Let's go."

They ran for the ship and did not care that the men on the dock preparing to set the ship free saw them. They startled one of them who was working to loosen the rope from its large metal cleat. He ran off with a shriek and they ran up the still tight rope back to the safety of their air duct lair.

There would be a lazy search the next day for a small and a humungous rat that ran on board. By then, the ship would be on its way to the next port of Paramaribo, Suriname.

CHAPTER SEVEN

The good ship, California Dreaming, was met by two tugboats when they approached Suriname. The tugs took them up the Suriname River to the small port where they would dock to load local rice to take to Colombia. Our two heroes watched from the shadows how the stacks of rice in large burlap sacks secured to wooden pallets were lowered into the hold. The fifty pallets of rice replaced one container of rubber tires from Brazil. The whole exchange took about four hours.

Caribbean music filled the air as the workers operated the loading cranes and organized the placing of the rice sacks. The music was an easy-going reggae sound.

"Do you hear that, Nuno? That's reggae music of Suriname. Despite being on the continent of South America, it really is a Caribbean country by culture."

"I have no idea what you're saying. Words like 'reggae' and 'Caribbean' mean nothing to me. But I like the music. It makes me want to sway and dance. Come on, Figo, show me how you dance."

"Oh, I can't dance. When I try it just seems like I'm shivering."

"Well, it's true that I can't tell if you're standing or sitting."

All work stopped by early evening. The tugs returned, and the ship was eased back down the river to the open sea. All was quiet and dark again.

"Looks like we're stuck on the ship without getting off." Figo stated the obvious.

"Considering how we almost missed our ship when we were in Brazil, I'm not upset about it. Unlike you, who is happy to roam the world like a homeless hobo, I am on a one-way trip to a specific destination. I have no interest in exploring every stop on the way."

"I thought you lynxes were supposed to be curious."

"We are, but only as tourists who go home after it's all over."

"As you like, but you're still the only lynx I met on a ship. Whatever you say, you are still very unusual. Most are happy to stay home and follow the latest football news. But you? No, you chose an adventure into the complete unknown. Just getting to the port in Lisboa is an adventure enough for anyone from Xisto."

"Enough said, Figo. I must say I am glad to have met you. Without you this trip would be nothing but boredom and dread."

"Hey, I'm getting hungry. Let's skip the kitchen tonight. Follow me."

Figo led Nuno to the great sacks of rice and he started to chew on a corner of one of them. After about five minutes, a small trickle of rice poured onto the floor.

"Ah, dinner time. It's simple but will do in a pinch. Come on. Don't just stand there."

"What? You expect me to eat that? Cooked rice is bad enough."

"Then I guess it's the kitchen trash can for you."

"Now wait a minute. What's this I smell?" Nuno leapt on top of a stack of rice sacks. One of the workers had left his unfinished lunch on a large plantain leaf. It was shrimp and dried fish cooked with flavors unlike anything else he had eaten. He quickly ate most of it before he thought of Figo, who was looking up at him with yearning in his eyes.

"Oh, all right. Climb up here and have some. Perhaps you can tell me what these wonderful flavors are that I am tasting."

Figo quickly scampered up the pile of sacks and helped himself to what was left.

"This makes me happy. I thought we might not have the chance to eat any Caribbean food on this trip. Now, let's see about the flavors. I can taste the allspice, nutmeg, and cinnamon right away. But there's something else. Yes, I taste the cloves, but there's something subtle that elevates this to a higher place. Oh, I know. It's ginger. That's what I'm tasting."

"You know your foods, Figo. I just know what tastes good and what doesn't. Certainly, uncooked rice is not one of them. Meat is all I care about."

"Well, Nuno, enjoy it while you can. It will be back to scrounging in the kitchen trash cans for the next few days."

The two of them bantered awhile, then wandered around the stacked containers before returning to their secret den while the sun started shining into the dark corners of the hold. The next night they indeed had to go to the kitchen and dig into the trash cans for something to get them through the next day.

It was always hit or miss, depending on the vagaries of what the cook made for dinner. Sometimes it was grilled chicken, much to Nuno's delight or it might be macaroni and cheese, much to his horror.

One such night, they were exploring the kitchen and the adjacent dining room. The light suddenly came on, catching Figo in the open. He was too stunned to move, like a deer in the headlights. The late night snacker grabbed the broom and tried to hit and kill Figo with the broomstick. He missed, but the second blow would land right on Figo's back.

Nuno happened to be behind the attacker and before he could think, he leapt on the back of the assailant and bit his ear. This forced the assailant to drop the broom and reach for the large heavy thing on his back. As he tried to grab Nuno, he tripped and fell. Figo ran out, closely followed by Nuno. The poor sailor was sitting on the kitchen floor holding his bleeding ear, alternating between yelling for help and many expletives about a demon attacking him from

behind.

Other sailors came running and helped him to his feet. They bandaged his ear, while listening to the description of the supposed demon who of course he never saw but could only feel clinging to his back. His description became worse every time he repeated it until Nuno became three meters tall and smelled like brimstone. Fortunately, it became so ridiculous that no one could believe him, though it was hard to explain the bite marks on his ear.

As for our two heroes, they decided that they would skip dinner the next night. Figo could eat the rice in the burlap sacks, but poor Nuno could only eat the remains of the dried rabbit Tiago prepared. Dried or not, it was awfully close to being past its due date. Fortunately, the ship was quickly approaching Colombia's port of Baranquilla.

CHAPTER EIGHT

Nuno could not sleep much that night. Between Figo full on dry rice snoring away and his own stomach growling like it was in some kind of cat fight, sleep eluded him. He was glad to hear the air horns of the tugs as they slowly maneuvered them up the Magdalena River to its berth at the Terminal Maritimo of Baranquilla, Colombia.

As they were docking, music blaring from the loudspeakers made Figo start to shiver in his version of dancing.

"Do you hear that, Nuno? That's Carlos Vives song, Pa Mayte."

"Don't know it, but I like it already." Nuno replied as he, too, started dancing.

"No, not like that. You dance the salsa here. Short little steps up and back, all the time swaying side to side." Figo showed Nuno how to dance the salsa, but to Nuno it just appeared to be more shivering as his feet were hidden by his fat body. But he tried to follow the instructions.

"I got the small steps forward and back, but I simply do not have the hips to sway side to side."

"Don't worry about it, Nuno, neither do I. I think it works best for those who walk on two paws."

"I think we just move to the music as the spirit moves us."

"Yes, you're right. Looking at the waning sunlight, I guess we only have an hour or two before night comes. Then, we can go out and explore new adventures."

"Figo, I will go out to explore, but no new adventures, please. I just want to get to California where the women folk love us from the old world."

"Really, Nuno? How do you know?"

"Well, I don't know, but I've been told."

"Interesting. Whenever I go there, I get ridiculed for my foreign accent."

They bantered and danced for a while until the music abruptly stopped and the dock lights came on, signaling that the workday was over, and night was quickly coming, the time for prowling.

The port of Baranquilla sat along the river where the large ships were tied up. On the other side of the dock flowed a small channel that entered a rectangular space of water for the river boats. All around this rectangle were the back sides of warehouses. At the mouth of the channel spread a large green space that had not been built on yet.

Our two friends made their way off the ship in search of a nice Colombian dinner. Figo knew just where to go. He led Nuno around the rectangle behind the warehouses all dark with no one working. The going was easy and eventually they found their way to a row of small traditional restaurants. As usual, they went to the back to search for recent additions to the trash bins.

After a few false starts, they found one that had hosted a big party that afternoon. In the trash bin, they found the remains of a whole pig that had been stuffed with rice, peas, onions, and spices. It had been cooked a long time in a clay oven. The locals called it Lechona.

"Look, Nuno, something for everyone. You have your meat and I have my peas and rice. And here is the pig's face. You could have fun scaring the dogs if you put the face on you like a mask."

"Are you crazy? I would never stick my head into that. Would need to spend hours cleaning my face." Nuno then proceeded to eat enough for two dinners, including the one he missed from the night before.

No person bothered them, but a dog came sniffing at the trash bin and started growling at the two he could smell inside. Nuno was tired of sitting in a heap of edible garbage and even more tired of hearing the dog outside who was not leaving.

"Nuno, do something about that damn dog."

"Gladly." And he leapt out and growled even fiercer than the dog who ran away whining.

"Well, that was easy."

They returned the way they came and as they approached the ship, their way was blocked by seven dogs, including the one they met earlier. He evidently went to find his pack of feral friends to get his revenge on being humiliated by a cat of all things.

They could not run past them to the ship, nor could they run back from where they came. They had to stand their ground. Figo could do nothing but huddle under Nuno. The dogs were snarling, showing their fangs. Nuno was not at all affected by their theatrics.

He yelled, "I have already seriously hurt one of you before. Now I can do it seven more times. He hissed and raised his back with his fur bristling out to make him look twice his size.

The dogs hesitated at this show of force, but then the one they met at the restaurant lunged at Nuno.

"Ah, you again. Well, take this." And razor-sharp claws ripped across the dog's face. It ran off whining even worse than before with a bloody face. "Next!"

The remaining six dogs attacked Nuno together. Each of them was at least twice Nuno's size, but he scratched, and bit faces and ears. The dogs pressed them back to the edge of the wharf. Little Figo came out a few times to bite a paw that came within reach. A dog almost got him in his maw, and Figo had to jump away, but he forgot how close he was to the water and fell in.

As he was falling, he yelled, "Help, Nuno! I can't swim!"

At this, Nuno had to stop fighting the remaining four dogs and leapt into the water to save Figo. As Figo was sinking, a paw swept

him up and onto Nuno's back.

"No, you are not leaving me until we get to California."

Figo gripped Nuno's wet fur, panting at his near-death experience. "What would I do without you? Thanks again."

But Nuno had a problem. The wharf was too high to climb out and he could not jump anywhere with his feet paddling in water. Fortunately, not too far away was the green space by the channel entrance. Nuno paddled over there slowly. The last time he found himself in water was when a bear startled him, and he had to jump into a pond to get away from the offensive creature.

Eventually, they made it. Nuno was exhausted from eating too much, the fight, and the swim. He lay panting by the water's edge while Figo cowered under a bush, shaking with fright.

After a while, he cried out to Nuno, "Come on, my friend, we need to return to the ship, and we have to walk all the way around this space of water. We might even have to fight those dogs again."

Nuno slowly raised himself and then swept Figo onto his back.

"You sit up there. It'll be faster."

Again, they walked around the back of the warehouses and as they turned the last corner, they could see the ship in the distance, but also the few remaining dogs of the pack that attacked them.

"Stay quiet. Let's see if we can sneak past them." Nuno kept to the shadows and slowly approached the ship unseen. But as he almost passed the dogs, one of them started to sniff the air and caught their scent. He started barking, causing the others to bark, too, though they had not yet understood what they were barking at or even why.

Since they were only a few meters away, Nuno thought quickly and told Figo to hold on tightly. He leapt onto the back of the closest dog. Viciously he clawed into its back, digging with his hind claws, and biting its neck. Fortunately for the dog, his neck was too big for Nuno to get a good grip with his jaws. The other dogs gathered around trying to save their comrade. Nuno had to let it go, while fending off the others.

Now Nuno was in no mood for a friendly neighborly spat. His wild cat's natural hatred for dogs came through and now he was fighting to kill and not just to scare away like he did the first time he met them. He went for the throat of one, but again the dog's neck was too thick to be broken. However, it could bleed.

There were only four dogs from the original seven. The others were off nursing their wounds. Within seconds, two of the four were in serious trouble and ran away leaving a trail of blood. Nuno attacked the third one with two swings of front claws followed by a bite at the neck. This was the last straw, and the last two ran away whining and snarling.

"Wow! You are simply great, Nuno. A real fighter."

"I hate dogs. I'll fight anything, except bears. You simply can't do anything with them. Come on, let's get back to the ship." Figo stayed clinging to Nuno's back. He decided that was the best mode of transportation for the rest of the time they would be together. They returned to their hiding place and fell into a deep sleep recovering from the tough evening they just survived.

CHAPTER NINE

The trip to Manzanillo, the main port on Mexico's west coast, would take four days. The highlight would be the twelve hours it would take to pass through the Panama Canal's fifty miles/eighty kilometers. Compared to this, the trip across the Caribbean to the canal's eastern entrance was quite fast.

When the ship entered the first canal lock and started to rise, Nuno panicked. He thought something was lifting the ship into the sky. His instinct was to grab on to something, but his claws had nothing to grip. Everything was metal. Figo was amused, as he had passed through this great modern marvel many times.

"Relax. Don't need to panic. We're going through the Panama Canal." Then, he started to explain what a canal is.

Nuno could only relax a bit, remaining nervous during the whole trip. As they approached the Pacific, the locks lowered them, causing Nuno to become nauseous. After that drama, they had three days to go up the west coast of Central America and Mexico.

For the four days of the trip, they had to eat the leftovers of whatever they could scrounge in the kitchen after midnight. Nuno felt he was getting fat and weak from the steady diet of what was found in trash cans. After he was weaned from his mother's milk, he had to stalk and pounce on everything he ate. Some days he had

to go hungry. This kept him a lean, hungry, hunting machine. He was anxious to get to California where he could eat a healthier diet of small mammals caught with honest effort, not like a thief sneaking into trash bins.

He also missed a tree with good thick bark where he could do a good scratch and sharpen his claws. Luckily, he had the recent chance to sharpen them on the hides of dogs. Yet, it was not quite the same thing, though the memory brought a smile to Nuno's face.

After another boring dinner from the dining room's trash can, they went to sleep. They were awakened by the tooting tugs as they pushed and pulled the ship into the Port of Manzanillo. They could not sleep when the ship docked, and the cranes worked on the containers. But one thing that made up for this inconvenience was the different music that the dock workers listened to.

As usual, Figo had something interesting to say about all the music they heard.

"Do you hear that, Nuno? That's Son Jarocho music. And they are playing the original version of La Bamba! Where you're going, everyone knows it as a song by Richie Valens, but no, this is the original."

"Do you know everything, Figo? What don't you know?"

"I know a lot, but not everything. I learned a lot from travelling around this world. Listening to what the locals say and keeping an open mind. You've learned a lot just on this short trip."

"Short? When will it ever end?"

"Well, you have learned a lot. For example, the next time you hear this song, you'll remember what old Uncle Figo told you."

"Uncle? How old are you?"

"Don't know, but with my experiences I feel I'm at least older than you."

"Well, maybe in world experiences you are. Those back home consider me an adolescent. So, yes, I have much to live and experience. I guess meeting you has been a big help in that regard."

"You can thank me whenever you want."

"Oh, all right, Figo. I'm thankful I didn't eat you right away. Really, I am, but I can't promise what will happen when we arrive in California."

"WHAT?"

"Just joking. I already consider you a friend. It's a point of honor with lynxes that we never eat our friends. In fact, I hope to convince you to join me in California and stop your vagabond life."

"That's not a funny joke at all. We rats never make jokes like that."

"To be fair, who would you make such a joke to? A grain of rice?"

"Ha. Very funny. I'll just pretend I didn't hear your so-called joke."

"Where's your sense of humor? Whatever. Never mind."

"Fine. Let me enjoy the rest of the song."

They stayed out of sight until the end of the workday. They managed to get a few hours of sleep before they could not ignore their growling stomachs. As darkness descended on the ship, they zigzagged between the containers on the way up to the deck and the docks. As they passed one of the newly placed containers, their sensitive noses could smell a peculiar scent.

"What is that smell, Figo? Not sure I like it."

"That, my friend, are avocados. You haven't lived until you ate one of those."

"There is nothing about that smell that makes me want to eat it. Come on, let's find some real food."

"Sure. Hope you like beans."

"Beans! I never can understand the humor of rodents."

"Oh, I'm sure we can find some meat for you. The Mexicans are a well-fed people. Being just a flesh-eater is so limiting."

Off the ship, they once again found themselves in the middle of a large port surrounded by stacks of containers with warehouses all around. Figo jumped onto Nuno's back and directed him how to leave the familiar metal forms to find a dock workers' restaurant.

After almost an hour of careful walking among the shadows of a sleeping port, they arrived at a row of small restaurants.

The trash bins of the first three restaurants only had rice, beans, and tortillas. But the fourth one had something special. Nuno dove right into the trash bin and discovered what his nose promised: the remains of a rabbit stew!

"Oh, Figo. You simply must try some of this. You haven't lived until you've eaten rabbit. The memories it brings!"

"I normally don't eat rabbit. I'm completely happy with beans, refried or otherwise."

"Great! I don't have to share." Nuno ate as if he had not eaten in weeks, which he felt was true. He had rabbit stew all over his face.

While Figo gingerly ate his dinner of beans, Nuno hid in the shadows behind the bins licking his paws and cleaning his face with great satisfaction. He liked the fact that those lucky enough to have beards can enjoy their meal a second time when they clean their face.

A brass band started to play in the restaurant. The two friends listened for a while before heading back to the ship. Nuno was getting excited about arriving in California to start his new life. It was their next stop. In two days, they would be there, the land of slow fat rabbits and lovely, adoring females.

CHAPTER TEN

After one more dinner of discarded half-eaten meals, the two friends were resting by the containers in the hold. Figo's curiosity got the better of him.

"Tell me, Nuno, how do you catch a rabbit?"

"Oh, now that is an interesting question. Let me show you. Pretend you're a rabbit, eating your seeds, grass, or whatever boring thing you eat. I'll move over here. Pretend I am in the shadows and you don't see me. I get really low to the ground, like this with my tail just slightly twitching."

"Now, that's silly. How can your little stub of a tail twitch?"

"Hey, it twitches, OK? Then, I pull my ears back flat against my head. I slowly move closer. And when I get this close, I pounce... Like this."

Nuno jumped on Figo holding him in his paws, careful not to let his deadly claws out.

"Then, if I'm in a jolly mood, I will play with you. For example, I might toss you in the air, like this." He flicked Figo into the air and caught him again as he came down while Figo was releasing a long-panicked squeak.

"I might just hold you under my claws. Pretend my claws are embedded in your body. You would be quivering in fear at this

point."

"I am! I am! Let me go!"

"That's exactly what they would be saying, but I don't let them go. Oh, no. For example, I might tear them in half. I've done that with field rats. Or I might bite the back of their necks until I feel their little neck bones snap in my mouth. Like this…"

"No! I get it. I get it. Let me go! I'm sorry I asked." Figo screamed as he felt sharp fangs grip on his neck.

"Hey, you asked, and I delivered."

"You get away from me!" Figo cried as he shivered from his near-death experience. He ran into a crevice and hid there.

"Come on now, Figo. I would never hurt you. Where is your sense of humor?"

After about twenty minutes, a hoarse squeak came out of the crevice. "In my world, everyone is trying to kill us. They smash us with shovels. Break our backs with a spring trap. Dissolve our insides with poison. But no one would ever 'play' with us like you do before ripping us apart."

"Come on, Figo. It's the only fun we get in life." That comment brought on another bout of distressed squeaking.

"Ah, wrong thing to say. Sorry. But we have similar lives. People crush us with their cars as we try to cross roads at night. We get our hind legs caught in metal traps with jaws. Then, we can only bite our leg off to escape. And we, too, eat poisoned meat and have our insides dissolve in great pain."

"Yes, but all of those things are not meant for you. You're just collateral damage. Killed by accident. After all, you're a so-called 'protected species', 'endangered' they say. But for us, it's open war."

"You're right, Figo. If you stay with me, I won't let any of that happen to you. You will have a big brother to protect you so you can live a long and happy life." Nuno whimpered, emotionally distraught from terrifying his new best buddy.

Figo came out of his crevice and slowly approached Nuno. "Yes,

I know." He scampered onto Nuno's back. He whispered into Nuno's big hairy ear, "But if you ever do that again, I will bite your ear like this." He took a strong bite on Nuno's ear.

"Ow! What are you doing, you crazy rodent?" And gave a great shake of his head, sending Figo sailing off into the air. But just as Figo was falling back down, Nuno caught him and flung him into the air again. This time Figo was laughing in the joy of knowing that he could always trust his silly big friend. They wrestled and played like this, laughing all the time for an hour. Actually, Figo could not really wrestle. The best he could do was grab onto a paw and pretend to bite it. But it was all good fun.

Finally, they had to rest.

"Just think, Nuno, after tomorrow night, we'll arrive in your golden California."

"Yeah. I guess that's what's making me get a bit wild and excited. I hope you decide to join me there."

"I don't know. I've become used to this vagabond life. I like adventure. But sometimes I yearn for a quiet normal life, too. Don't know. We'll see. I still have a day to think about it."

"You can try it and if it's not for you, you can always find another ship to take you to places unknown. And you can always come back, too. You will always be welcome wherever I am."

"That's great. That really is, Nuno. I just might take you up on that."

They wandered around the containers for a few more hours and crawled back to their hidden nest in the metal air vent where they made their home for the past weeks. Figo slept normally, as any other night. But Nuno purred and snored as he dreamt of all the wonderful things he would find at his destination. He, like so many millions before him on the day before they would arrive in California, dreamed about how much better life would soon be.

Late the next night, Nuno refused to eat from the dining room trash can. No, his next meal, he decided, would be on land, even if it, too, had to be from a trash can. It would at least be a Californian trash can.

The ship was slowing down. The familiar fog horns of the tugboats sounded as they sought to secure the much bigger freighter. After a while, they felt the ship gently hit the old rubber truck tires tied to the side of the dock to cushion the force of the docking ship. The SS California Dreaming was secured to the dock. But there was only silence to greet them this time. The sun still had not come up. It was still too early for the regular dock workers to start unloading the containers from the smaller tramp freighters.

Nuno did not care about music. He flicked Figo on his back and scampered up to the deck and down the rope onto the dock. He stopped and breathed deeply the early air of his new home. He had arrived!

CHAPTER ELEVEN

Since Figo did not immediately jump off Nuno's back, apparently, he had made up his mind to join Nuno on his new California adventure. Meanwhile Nuno was finding a way out of the port by following the chain-link fence, looking for a hole to slip through like with all the other ports he had been to before. But this port was much better maintained.

After a few hours, the only exit he could find was through the front gate that admitted trucks to pick up their containers. Though the sun had not risen, there were plenty of lights on everywhere, including the big headlights of the trucks. Nuno tried to wait for a break, but there was none. He got as close to the open gate as he could slink, but then he just had to make a run for the darkness on the other side.

While the guard was checking the credentials of the truck driver, Nuno slipped behind and out. The truck driver noticed and pointing to Nuno, said to the guard, "Hey, you have a dog loose."

Before the guard could turn around, Nuno disappeared into the early morning shadows.

Figo whispered into Nuno's ear, "I would like to point out the music from the guard house is Creedence Clearwater Revival and the music from the truck is Social Distortion, two excellent examples of American rock and roll."

"Not now, Figo! We need to find a place to hide before the sun rises."

Nuno remembered the advice from his friend's father to always keep the ocean to his right. Just as the sun was rising, he found a water drainage pipe leaking a small stream of water into the ocean. Staying to the dry side of the little stream of water, they laid down and rested.

"I guess I decided to join you, Nuno. Do you know where you're going?"

"Yes, I know where I'm going."

"Excellent. Next question: do you know how to get there?"

"Yes. Go south with the ocean always on our right."

"How will you know when you reach your destination?"

"I'll know when we get there. It's the getting there part that worries me. We have about five days of traveling through uninterrupted towns and cities before we arrive. Do you have any ideas?"

"I suggest we travel along the beach where it meets the land. Our shadows would clearly stand out under the bright moonlight if we walked on the beach. There will be many trash cans along the way to scavenge something to eat and I suppose drainage pipes like this to hide in during the day."

"As usual, Figo, you're always full of great ideas. Glad you decided to join me."

"Yeah, I guess I did. I can always go back to a ship if I get bored."

"Let's make sure you don't get bored."

They slept through the day. When night finally came, they were very hungry. So, first they found food in the trash bin of a dive bar and grill for sailors. The steaks were so big that there were many half-eaten parts to fill any lynx's stomach. There was plenty of everything else to keep a battalion of rats happy.

Continuing along the edge of the beach of a city appropriately named Long Beach, it took them all night to pass through it. They found another drainage pipe that was big enough for someone to walk upright through it. It was time for sleeping and they crept into the dark middle part.

Their sound sleep was interrupted by the squeal of a small group of young boys who had stumbled upon them while passing through their favorite way to the beach. One of them poked at Nuno with a long stick. Nuno did not take kindly to that and rose with a great growl. He threatened them, hoping they would run away.

This did not work. Instead they started to throw stones at him. Nuno reared back on his rear haunches preparing to leap onto them.

"No, Nuno! You can't hurt them. If you do, the whole population of southern California will be hunting for us. Let me take care of this."

Figo ran directly at them with the loudest rat squeal he could make, showing his teeth. This caused panic with the boys who ran as fast as they could out and away.

"See? That is how you deal with them. You might like to know there is a quote from a famous Japanese novel called I Am a Cat, by Natsume Sōseki that a Japanese rat friend told me about once. It goes something like this: 'The whole world knows that cats are smarter than eight-year-old boys.'"

"The whole world, huh? Except them, I guess."

"Yeah, the Japanese adore cats. You'd love it there."

"Once we arrive at our destination, I doubt I'll travel anywhere far again."

Nothing bothered them for the rest of the day. Night came again, and they continued their journey. Sometimes they had to climb over rocks. At other times, they passed by cliffs.

Once they slept in a cave below the cliffs. When night came, as they were leaving the small cave to continue their trip south, a homeless man was entering the cave to sleep at the end of his busy day of panhandling. There was a brief moment of confusion until he stepped out of the way to let them pass. Though he certainly had an unclear mind, he was no eight-year-old boy.

Other than this, there were no more adventures for the rest of their journey. It was about five days when they passed south of Corona del Mar and Newport Beach. The non-stop houses ended, and a large wilderness spread before them that reached up into the hills to the east and away from the beach.

"This must be it! This must be what Tiago told me about!" Nuno exclaimed loudly.

There were shrubs and trees, natural springs and streams for fresh water, and plenty of places for a lynx to sleep in peace. Most importantly, the area was hopping with rabbits, squirrels, and small birds.

After climbing to the top of the nearest hill, Nuno looked down upon all of this and sighed, "I'm home at last!"

CHAPTER TWELVE

"You know, Figo, this place reminds me of Xisto. It's Xisto by the sea."

"I can see that." Figo replied. "But we have to find a safe place to sleep."

"Let's start exploring."

As soon as the sun set, they set out. It was a large area with no human habitation. There were a few trails that crossed the otherwise undeveloped area. These had the scent of people's shoes. They knew they could not be close to those. But fortunately, these human footpaths were not many.

There was a road that separated the area from the sea. Neither Nuno nor Figo saw any reason to go there. There was one other road that cut through from east to west. This road had a few houses and stores along it. But behind them rose a high hill with cliffs to another expansive space that lacked trees but was full of ravines and most importantly rabbits. This undeveloped space was big enough for a lynx to roam without coming in contact with human life if he did not want to, and he definitely did not want to.

As they searched for a suitable place to settle into, they met animals that he had never seen before, like squirrels who lived in trees. Nuno tried them and liked them. There was another animal

that appeared to be a cross between a squirrel and a rat. They lived in holes in the ground. Nuno liked them, too. But the rabbits, oh the rabbits. Now they were worth the trip. They were as slow-witted and fat as Tiago told him.

As they explored the edges of their domain, where the houses and their green lawns met the brushland, Nuno came across another type of animal. Once when Figo was at a distance from Nuno, exploring holes in the ground, Nuno looked for him. When he saw Figo in the distance, he was shocked to see a smaller version of himself, about half his size, creeping closer to Figo ready to pounce.

Nuno first thought that this would be a nice meal, bigger than anything else he found. But the eerie similarity made him think twice. In fact, he was confused. In a state of confusion, sometimes it was best to ask clarifying questions. So, Nuno crept closer to this feline hunter and when he was right next to her, he asked, "How's it going, sister?"

The house cat was not really particularly good at hunting and was not even hungry. She was just following a long-buried instinct to stalk and pounce on unsuspecting rodents. Suddenly, she was surprised by a giant version of herself with no taming influences, like a genteel Roman maiden meeting a barbarian in the forest while picking berries.

She did what any other fat and happy house cat would do. She hissed and ran away to the safety of her house and humans. Figo witnessed this encounter of the panicked cat with a confused Nuno.

"Figo, what was that all about? I just asked her a simple question, and she got all hissy and ran off. I mean, I could have pounced on her and we would have had a big dinner. But, oh no, I decided to be friendly."

"Nuno, you can't eat cats. That would be like me eating mice. Don't get me wrong. I hate cats. We have been enemies almost as long as humans have tried to exterminate us. In fact, I believe humans befriended cats specifically to help them kill us. I would have relished the thought of eating a cat. Oh, the delicious irony of that! But no, even us rats have a sense of dignity."

"Thanks. You answered my question. So, I did do the right thing. Sometimes I'm not too sure. In the future, I'll try to befriend these distant cousins of mine."

"But look. If you want to make friends with them, just do it without me around. I wouldn't trust them as far as I could throw them, and that's not far at all."

"Don't worry. I would only make friends with a cat that is as big as me and likes rodents, but in a good way. I suppose there will be none like that around. I would not even trust a fellow lynx. Hey, do you think there are any lynxes around here? Tiago told me they live far to the north and I would never meet any here.

"He did mention there are occasionally huge cats around here who are 4 or 5 times bigger than me but are usually further east than here. In the mountains, Tiago said. When I think of it, I'd really rather not meet them. My fur rises on my back when I think of them. Tiago also told me they are active at night, too."

"You also have to be wary of large dogs about twice your size."

"Dogs don't worry me."

"No, Nuno. These dogs are called coyotes and they are wilder than any dog you have met. They are dangerous. But fortunately, they only come out during the day and only hunt singly or in pairs. Best to avoid them."

"I avoid even dogs, but I'm not afraid of them. But the giant mountain lynx worries me. Tiago told me they almost never appear out of the mountains much farther to the west. But still, I agree we must keep our wits about us. You almost lost it to that silly cat."

Figo decided he would stay much closer to Nuno. They continued to search for a permanent home. A few days later they found a small cave in one of the ravines that fit their list of needs. It was far from humans and their traffic. It was close to fine hunting grounds, and the ravine had a small stream feeding into it.

Except for a brief encounter between Figo and a hawk that Nuno put a stop to, life was fine for the two friends. Nuno was back in his fighting form thanks to no longer eating cooked food from trash bins and having to catch his meal with wit and speed. Figo never changed, no matter what he ate.

Some weeks later, Nuno said to Figo, "Everything is fine. I'm satisfied with this place. But I do miss some good female companionship. Since there are no lynxes anywhere near here, I really must consider the next best thing, which are cats. But they are so small. It would be like having a lynx cub as a friend, and that's simply ridiculous. But still..." His voice trailed off.

"I wouldn't mind some companionship myself. But who would dare have me when I have the smell of lynx all over me? Fortunately, I only ever think about it for about a few weeks twice a year."

"Hey! What's wrong with the 'smell of lynx'?"

"I'm used to it now, but for those who aren't, it's enough to make them quiver in fear."

"Shall I drop you into the stream and wash my smell off?"

"No. I can't swim. I'm used to being alone. Let's concentrate on finding you a special friend who doesn't mind sharing you with me."

"Oh, that's sweet, Figo. Not sure how you can help me, except by just sticking around and being my friend."

CHAPTER THIRTEEN

Every few days they would meet house cats practicing their almost lost hunting skills. And after the encounter with the hawk, Figo decided to stick with riding on Nuno's back. One day they followed the greener part of their range under the highway to the eastern side. This part was surrounded by four-story office buildings. The trees and the bushes gave them plenty of places to hide if need be. But there was no one there at the prowling hours.

Nuno saw a rabbit and started to stalk it. He inched closer and closer with Figo holding on tight to Nuno's fur. Just as Nuno leaned back on his haunches to pounce, another cat almost as big as him pounced first, grabbed the rabbit, and disappeared into the bushes.

Startled, he could only stand up and watch his prey disappear in the jaws of a true hunter, but even faster than him. This vexed him. He continued and found another rabbit to stalk. And again, just before he could pounce, the same cat pounced first and disappeared into the bushes with the rabbit. Nuno was now very irritated. He tried for a third rabbit and again the same thing happened. This time he yelled at the disappearing cat, "Hey, you can only eat one at a time!"

Again, he found yet a fourth rabbit. He stalked the rabbit in classic lynx fashion. Just as he was prepared to pounce, he was pounced on from behind by that same big cat, sending Figo flying. This knocked Nuno on his side. He was also being bit. He noticed that the cat's claws were not out, and the bites were something he remembered doing to his siblings when they were all cubs.

He broke free and took a good look at this strange cat, staring straight at him. The cat walked up to him, gave him a slow blink of the eyes, and put her nose right up to his. This was a sign of affection between new cat acquaintances. Nuno realized that this was not a typical house cat. She was the size of a lynx, but not a lynx. And most importantly, she was a she-cat.

"Who are you? And why are you teasing me like this?" He asked her.

"Just my way of being friendly. Not seen a he-cat as big as you for a long time. And your accent? What is it? You're not from around here, are you?"

"As a matter of fact, I'm not. I arrived about a month ago by a ship from Portugal. I have a special Xisto accent."

"Xisto? That's where my dad was from. He returned there a few years ago."

"You mean Tiago? Was that his name?"

"Yeah, I think so. We just called him 'Tigre'."

"Yes, I know him. He was the one who told me about this place and how to get here."

"Why did he leave us?"

"In the home country, we have to take care of our parents and his were getting old. I was wondering why you're so much bigger than other cats."

"My mother was from Maine. She was as big as Tigre. I think they call her a Coon Cat from Maine or a Maine Coon Cat. I never knew either one very well. Here, once we are old enough to leave the den, we go and don't look back. So, I knew my father for about six months. He never talked much and never spoke about his past. Enough about him. Let's talk about you. I like your accent. And I like what I see."

"And what do you see?"

"I see a manly big cat with a lovely foreign accent and very attractive long hairy ears."

"Now look, I'm not a rabbit." He stammered as she rubbed her side up against his.

"Oh, no, you're definitely not," she replied with a bit of a purr. "I'll have more interest in you than a rabbit, whom I've forgotten after an hour of eating it. I would like to keep my interest in you for an exceptionally long time."

"Sorry. I'm not used to such an aggressive she-cat so soon after meeting. Where I come from, they like to think they are ladies with a reputation to protect. We need to pursue them and even fight for them with other men cats. They love that, but when they're ready, they drop all pretense of being a lady. Then Mother Nature takes over. Let's start with your name."

"My name? Which one? I have three."

"Three? I only have one, but it does have eight words. It's my family name. It goes like this: Nuno Espinoza de Campos Leitão Bacalhau Camões Felizardo. You can just call me Nuno. What's yours?"

"I can only pronounce the 'Nuno' and the 'de', I'm afraid. So, Nuno it is. My first name is the one my parents gave me. It's Electra."

"Well, that's a sensible practical name."

"Yes, but don't interrupt, sweetie. Then, there is the one my friends call me: Euterpe."

"I like that. It's peculiar yet dignified in some way. What's your third name?"

"Oh, that one? That's the one I can't tell you. It's my secret."

"Come on. Who has a secret name? Names are for sharing."

"Well, maybe one day I'll tell you. You know when we get to know each other better...." Her voice trailing off to a purr.

"Fine. What should I call you? Are we family or friends?"

"Whoa, not so fast, cowboy! We're not family yet. Let's start with being friends. You can call me 'Terpsie' for now."

"Terpsie! Where did you get that?"

"Look, call me anything you like, Big Ears."

Just then, Figo gave Nuno's front paw a good kick, which felt like a fly had landed. "Hey, don't forget to introduce me!" Figo squeaked.

Terpsie asked Nuno, "Will you eat that rodent, or shall I?"

"No! You will not eat Figo. He's my friend, and we travelled from Portugal together."

"Oh, come on, what kind of cat worthy of the name befriends rodents?"

"First, I am not a cat. I am a lynx and proud of it. Second, if you ever harm Figo, you will learn the difference between a cat and a lynx, especially an Iberian one. So, if you want us to get along, you must respect Figo as my dear friend. We've been through a lot. Otherwise this, whatever this is, will end before it even starts. Am I clear?"

"Are you serious? Oh, I see you are serious. All right, fine. You old world he-cats are so romantic about everything. I guess even about rodents, too. Fortunately, there are plenty of rabbits, squirrels, burrowing owls, scrub jays, chipmunks here that I guess I can skip one rodent. What's his name, so I don't eat him by mistake?"

"Mademoiselle, my name is Figo and I can speak for myself."

"'Mademoiselle'? What kind of word is that?"

"Well, madame if you prefer."

"'Madame'? That's even worse. I might be many things, but I'm no 'madame'. You need to go to certain parts of LA to find them. Just call me Terpsie and nothing fancy."

"Fine, Terpsie. Pleased to meet you. I was hoping Nuno would find someone special soon. He has been getting very lonely lately. It's a kind of loneliness that I can't help with."

"Oh, lonely, is he? Well, I know exactly the cure for that."

CHAPTER FOURTEEN

Nuno was cured of his loneliness and not too long afterwards he had created his first family. Six kittens were added to the world, and he was a happy lynx. Terpsie stayed with the kittens, sleeping, and nursing all day long. Nuno would bring back rabbits, squirrels, and whatever else he could catch to feed everyone. Figo would stay with Terpsie and play with the kittens, keeping them inside the small cave they called home, while their mother could sleep and recover.

When Nuno was not busy hunting, he would play with the kittens, too. Giving them great licks that would produce little purrs. For their part, the kittens would climb all over Nuno and fall asleep in whatever curve of his body they could find. Terpsie could not believe that their father did not disappear as soon as they were born like normal cats do. Then, of course, Nuno was no normal cat.

One day, Nuno was away hunting. The kittens were already one month old and started to wander to the entrance of the little cave to explore their new world. Figo had difficulty keeping them from leaving the cave while Terpsie was sleeping. Their mewing caught the attention of a passing coyote and followed their sound to the cave.

The kittens still did not know the meaning of the word 'enemy' and were curious. Figo understood very well what a dangerous

enemy was and, squeaking frantically, tried to keep them in the cave. But he was one, and they were six. The coyote grabbed one in his mouth and in two bites swallowed the poor kitten whole. At this point, Terpsie leapt out of the cave onto the neck of the coyote, fighting to the death to protect her young. At this, the kittens understood fear for the first time and willingly let Figo push them inside.

Urgent growls and cries filled the air as the two fought. Though one was only hungry, the other was a mother fighting for her young. Yet, the coyote was much bigger than Terpsie and was getting the better of her. Just when Terpsie thought she could not hold on any longer, Nuno arrived.

He dropped his rabbit and pounced on top of the coyote. While flaying the coyote's back with his hind claws, he bit the back of his neck. This was too much for the coyote. He struggled to knock Nuno off. He finally did, but not until suffering serious wounds. He ran off trailing blood.

Nuno let him go to tend to poor Terpsie, who had bites of her own to deal with. Nuno licked them until they stopped bleeding. Her wounds would heal, but not without leaving scars.

Nuno stayed with them in the cave in case the coyote would come back. But a few days later when he noticed vultures circling overhead, he felt it might be safe to search for food again. But just to make sure he approached to where the vultures circled. Just as he thought, the coyote bled to death under a tree about fifty meters away.

The coyote's carcass had already started to stink. Nuno went in search of fresh food. They had not eaten in two days. Luckily, the rabbit population remained healthy and they could eat again like normal. Things returned to normal, minus one kitten.

At the age of two months, it was time that the kittens learned how to survive on their own. Terpsie would take them on short trips outside the cave to teach them how to hunt. The kittens already learned to be wary of animals bigger than their parents.

Figo would tag along. Fortunately, the kittens were growing up and considered him as another smaller but older kitten. Terpsie had come to love the little rodent as a real friend.

She first taught her kittens how to stalk and pounce, starting with small things like beetles. The kittens thought it was great fun. They were naturals at it. They pounced on many beetles, never killing them. They loved the game, pouncing, holding it in their paws, letting it go, and repeating.

On one such outing, Figo noticed a shadow falling on him. His instinct quickly kicked in and he leapt behind a nearby rock just as a hawk swept down. Terpsie was too far away to protect the kitten who still did not understand what shadows from above meant. Terpsie leapt into the air, but the golden eagle already was far above with a kitten in its talons. Disaster fell once again on Nuno's family.

Terpsie gathered her remaining kittens by a rock and cried for her loss. With his keen hearing, Nuno heard and ran to them. He licked her face and ears but could not console her. She had lost two kittens in two months.

Later, they discussed the idea that maybe this Eden was not so ideal and maybe should find another place. But they knew there was no other. They were surrounded by one of the largest suburbs of the world. Nuno did not want to raise his kittens eating people's garbage like thieves. Besides, back in Xisto he had lost three siblings before he was six months old. It was a fact of life living in Nature.

They decided that Terpsie would do the hunting and Nuno would teach them how to grow up in the tough wilds of Orange County. Being bigger, stronger, and wilder, he could protect them better. Even so, another kitten pounced on the wrong snake and was bitten. She died within an hour, most painfully. Eventually, the remaining three kittens survived.

There was one that was Nuno's favorite. She looked just like her mother with all the colors in her fur, a completely blond stomach, with her upper parts covered in black, brown, grey with a white chin. She had all the other attributes of her mother, very furry feet, a big fluffy tail, and the marking of an 'M' on her forehead.

She loved climbing on the back of her father and riding him like a horse. She would tug on his very hairy ears to indicate which direction she wanted him to go. Nuno was never happier to oblige. They were inseparable. They went hunting together, and she learned how to catch the fast weaving rabbits almost as well as Nuno could. Even as she passed the six-month mark, when most cats leave their litter, she had no interest in leaving her beloved foreign father.

As for Figo, he was growing older, and he knew it. He no longer had the energy to wrestle with kittens now six times his size. He also could not bring himself to bring more sorrow to his adopted family if one day they found him cold and motionless. So, he took Nuno aside.

"I must tell you, Nuno, I am so happy that you have found your new home and started such a wonderful family. I feel that it's my family, too."

"You know we are happy to have you with us. You have been a real help and friend. And you certainly are a part of our family."

"Yeah, we had some real adventures together." And they reminisced about their crazy trip by ship and experiences at the various ports along the way. Finally, Figo brought up the real reason for their chat.

"Well, that's just the thing, Nuno. I feel it's time for me to start another adventure. I have done all I can here. It's been almost a year. It's time for me to move on."

"What are you talking about?! You're part of the family. You can't leave!"

"Nuno, your two male kittens have grown, and they already have left. We haven't seen them for several weeks now. You have one still staying behind. But even she one day will leave soon. Then, it would be time for you and Terpsie to start a new family."

"So? That doesn't mean you have to leave. No! I won't let you."

"Nuno, do you remember when we first arrived and had not even left the ship? I agreed that I would join you only if I could leave when I felt the time had come. Well, the time has come. I really must start this journey."

"Yes, I remember. All right, fine! I'll join you. We'll go off to China or wherever you want. Off to more adventures, just like we did before." Nuno said with desperation.

"No, my friend. This is a journey only I can make. I must go alone."

"Of course, I can't stop you. But how can I persuade you to stay?"

"You can't. I have heard that Time waits for no one. I can no longer wait, either."

"What are you talking about? Time?"

"Look, I won't leave right away. OK?"

"Stay as long as you possibly can."

"Fine." And they stopped talking about it.

But two late afternoons later, Nuno awoke and could not find Figo. He knew the time of their separation had come. He cried loudly into the empty night. He cried for his dear friend. Even Terpsie could not console him, and she was sad too that Figo was gone.

CHAPTER FIFTEEN

Nuno could not grieve for long. He had a family to feed. Hunting furry scrubland and forest folk soon took his mind off his loss. He took his daughter with him on these hunting trips, the only one still with her parents.

She loved her father and learned quickly how to hunt for herself. She knew which prey were worth the energy and which not. Others were to be avoided at all costs. One such animal to avoid was the rattlesnake.

One hot day she wandered away from Nuno and discovered a strange round flat animal. It was coiled in a pile of its own body, sunning itself. She came up close to have a sniff. Suddenly, it woke up, raising its head. It made an evil sounding rattle from its tail.

She froze, not sure what to do. She knew no fear, except for coyotes. She slowly approached the snake, her curiosity taking over her common sense. It had such a curious smell, after all. Just as the snake was preparing to strike, Nuno rushed from the bushes nearby and growled loudly. The snake turned to see what this new threat was and struck at the quickly advancing Nuno.

Nuno leapt out of range of the striking snake and before it could recoil, Nuno was on it. Biting its neck quickly put an end to the snake. He was quite upset with his daughter, but also proud that she was not a fearful cat. He explained that she should never approach anything that looked like the now dead snake. He told her to take a bite so that she would learn that they did not even taste good.

When they returned home, she would ride on Nuno's back like Figo used to do. Nuno transferred all his love for Figo to his daughter. They went everywhere and did everything together.

Terpsie was not jealous, but she knew that one day soon their daughter would also leave and that might break Nuno's heart a second time. But there was nothing she could do or say to him. As for Nuno, he just banished from his mind her explanations and warnings. He did not want to even think about it.

It was because of this that he refused to name her. He had the superstitious idea that if he named her, she would be grown up and then leave. But without a name she would stay the little kitten that she was clearly no longer to anyone else. He simply called her 'Kitten'.

As for Terpsie, she did not mind too much. She had never met a male who stuck around like Nuno did. As long as their nameless daughter stayed, Nuno would, too. But if she left, then Nuno would probably do the same soon after. Male cats, big or small, were never known to be monogamous.

Terpsie knew all too well that there were many jealous females lurking about, especially the bored rich ones who lived up in the houses on the hills around their open space. She knew that she had the best male cat in all of southern California. She was also receiving messages from her body that it would be soon time to start another family and would need Nuno's undivided attention.

Meanwhile, Nuno would continue hunting with the nameless kitten on his back who was now getting heavier every day. Sometimes they would meet her siblings in the wild space. Nuno would walk up to them and touch noses. They would stifle a purr trying to look all tough and grown up to their dad. Their sister would jump down and wrestle with them for a while until they remembered they were no longer kittens and break it off with a serious bat on her ears. Then they would part ways until the next time their paths would cross in the large but limited expanse of their domain.

At six months old, the kittens were already as large as normal grown cats. Yet, Nuno insisted on carrying his favorite kitten on his back. This slowed him down, but he did not mind. Kitten riding on his back reminded him of his dearly missed friend Figo, who he knew he would never see again.

In the early evening, he liked hunting for rabbits near the office park at the eastern edge of his territory. Kitten said, "Come on, Dad, we have enough for today."

"No, just one more. Can't have too many. I remember still how in the old country we never had enough. Some days we would have nothing to eat at all. Look, there's one. I'll catch him. Hold on!"

And he chased a particularly fat rabbit. He could not run so fast with Kitten on his back, but still was gaining on the rabbit. It ran across the road to the safety of the bushes on the other side. Nuno followed in hot pursuit. Just then, a car was passing by and, before Nuno could react, hit him on his hind quarters. Kitten flew into the air and into the bushes on one side of the road. Nuno was knocked onto the other side.

Nuno struggled away with his hind hip broken, not understanding what even happened. Kitten was panting heavily in a bush, unhurt but completely stunned and dazed. The car stopped by the side of the road and a woman got out.

Her husband sitting in the passenger seat called out, "What are you doing? We hit something. So what?"

"Frank, what is wrong with you?"

"It looked like a coyote. It'll bite you."

"I must see what we just did. Ah, it's a cat. It's stunned. We have to take it to a vet and make sure nothing is wrong with it."

"Oh, come on! Leave it alone."

"Are you crazy? This is someone's cherished pet. We have to get it back to its owner. What if someone hit our Fluffie? Wouldn't you want someone to try to find us? Throw me the blanket in the back

seat."

"For crying out loud, Fran. OK, here."

Fran wrapped Kitten up in the blanket and got in the back seat. "Take us to our vet's animal hospital."

Kitten disappeared into the back of the car and Nuno's most cherished being in the whole world disappeared down the road. Nuno half crawled and half staggered back into the middle of the road, looking mournfully at the disappearing car and gave a most heart wrenching, baleful cry. His sorrow and pain blinded him.

Another car swerved and missed him but went off the road stopping on the grass. The driver rolled down the window to see better what he almost hit. He opened the door to take a closer look.

"That cat was hit by a car. Let's take it to a veterinarian."

The passenger gasped, "Oh, my god, Joshua, it's a lynx! They're an endangered species. If the police come by and see us, they'll surely arrest us."

"What? Clearly, I didn't hit it."

"Yes, but it would appear that you did. Better get out of here!" And the car sped back onto the road and away.

Terpsie heard Nuno's cries and raced to him. She helped him back on his feet. Leaning on her all the way, they slowly returned to their den. She asked Nuno what happened, and his replies made no sense. He could barely put words together; his mind was so distraught. He laid down and cried for hours through the night. All Terpsie could do was hold him in her paws and lick his injuries.

CHAPTER SIXTEEN

Nuno laid in their den moaning for days. He would not eat anything and would only crawl to drink from the stream running close by. His pain of losing Kitten was far worse than his physical pain of being hit by the car. The pain from his growling empty stomach was a distant third. He was wasting away. He refused to eat all the nice things Terpsie brought him: a rabbit, a squirrel, a scrub jay, even a burrowing owl. He refused to eat anything.

Terpsie was afraid she might lose Nuno and that would break her heart. She tried to reason with him with logic. He would have lost Kitten one way or the other. Things would be better for her, taken out of the wild, and cared for in a nice home. That just produced more feeble moans.

She tried being angry with him. "Get up and be a man! Get up and live! Come on, try to stand up." This would stop the moans but otherwise produced no other results.

She tried to purr sweet nothings into his ear, holding him in her paws. She tried everything and could not think of anything else. It had been a week, and Nuno was dangerously thin. He could not protect them from a coyote if one came by.

This thought gave Terpsie an idea. One night, she leapt up with her fur standing on end and her tail twitching. "Nuno! A coyote! A

coyote is coming for us. Please do something. You know I can't defend us on my own. Help!"

At this, Nuno struggled to his feet and growled into the darkness. He took a few weak steps out of their den, though he could hardly stand up. "Where is it? Where?"

"There! Over by those bushes."

Nuno tried to stagger over to the bushes.

"No, don't go there. Just try to scare it away with your growls."

Nuno growled with the most fearsome growls a starving lynx could make.

After some minutes, Terpsie told him, "It's run away. You've scared it off. Come on, Nuno, you must eat something. Otherwise, how can you defend us from even a lost pigeon? If that coyote attacked us, we would have been done for. Here, eat these rabbits I caught just a while ago."

Nuno ate the rabbit. Terpsie found a way to make him eat. She appealed to his sense of honor to protect his family. That cut through everything else. Once he finished one rabbit, his hunger drove him to eat the second one. And so, he started eating again.

After a few more weeks of resting and eating, Nuno's hip was healed to the point that he could walk, though slowly and unevenly. He certainly could not run and had to rely on Terpsie for eating. All he could catch were beetles. But no one wanted to eat them.

It was way too early for the pain of losing Kitten to go away. Sometimes he would sit for hours staring into the distance, not seeing anything, suffering the pain for his loss in silence. Terpsie would try to cheer him up by chattering about all kinds of little things. All he would do was to give her a lick on the face, remaining in silence.

He appreciated her attempts to cheer him up, to care for him, to be there for him. Most of all, he appreciated her bringing him back to life again. Nuno decided that he had to live for her sake. He had to be strong for her.

So, life returned to normal, except Nuno stayed close to the den, trying to walk further every day, while Terpsie would do the hunting. He was always worried about her. While she was away, he would try to listen for her in the dark distance. He would listen for any dangers and threats. With his big ears he could just barely hear her creeping through the brushland that was their home.

Eventually life returned to normal, except for Nuno's handicap and his loss of his normal joy for life. Terpsie's love and care would make him forget sometimes his sense of loss. Though he could no longer hunt, he could walk with a limp. When he tried to run, the best he could do was a short slow shuffle.

In time, they even had a few more litters of kittens. They brought joy to his heart again, but none could replace the Kitten. None would ride on his back as he would roam his kingdom teaching them how to hunt for rabbits like he did with her. Even if he wanted to, his hip could not support any extra weight. Instead, he would just lay in the den, while Terpsie did the hunting, and let the little ones climb all over him, finding a nook anywhere on his body to take a nap.

Two years passed. When the last of the young ones from the last litter left to start their own lives, Terpsie sat down next to Nuno in silence. She clearly wanted to say something but was considering how to say it. Nuno waited patiently.

Finally, she spoke, "Nuno, my friend, I must tell you we are no longer young anymore. That last litter we had was our last. I am too old to have kittens anymore. We will just have ourselves to care for."

Nuno sat in silence, also with something to say but considering how to say it.

He answered, "As I have said often, I am ever so grateful for your care and love. I would not have even survived without you. I will be by your side until our last days. During these past few months, I've been doing a lot of thinking. We are still healthy. We can still move about. I want to give you a gift, something to show my gratitude.

"You have asked me a lot about the old country, the country where your father came from. There were many reasons why I left, and I am so glad I did for no other reason than meeting you. And my dear friend Figo and my dearest Kitten…." His voice trailed off, remembering the great sadness in his heart.

Terpsie sat in silence waiting for Nuno to recover. He continued, "My dear Terpsie, now that having another family is behind us, I want to take you back to my home, where we would always have a large extended family.

"It is not an easy journey and will take maybe two months. We will have to eat our food from cans, the refuse of people. We will need to be exceptionally careful of many possible dangers. But I have done it before, and I know we can do it. The trip back is easier and shorter. The ship goes directly across the ocean to the old country not stopping at many ports like I had to do to get here. What do you think about it? If you have to think it over, I'd understand. If you don't want to go, that would be fine, and we'll stay here. It is a big decision to…"

Terpsie interrupted him, "Stop! No more. I would love to go. I have never been out of this little patch of land. I have always dreamed about it, never thinking it would happen. We'll leave tomorrow."

CHAPTER SEVENTEEN

The next night, when the moon started to rise, they had one more feast of fresh rabbit. After a little rest to digest, Nuno led Terpsie back the way he originally came those many years before. Though he could walk, he felt a slight pain with every step he took. He knew if he encountered danger, he would not be able to run or leap to safety. He had to rely on his wits to keep them safe.

Terpsie walked slowly to stay by him. Nuno felt the irony that he was now like Figo to Terpsie. He knew the way and the ins and outs of the trip but would have to rely on her if they ever had to get into a fight with dogs or boys.

Though Terpsie's heart was full of the excitement of a new adventure, Nuno's heart was filled with sadness of leaving his new home and Kitten behind forever. For him, it was a long and dangerous trip back to the place he had escaped from so long ago. But it was the right thing to do. He wanted to be buried beside the slate hills of Xisto when that time came.

Back to the drainpipe that let the stream flow under the Pacific Coast Highway, he led her to the cliffs over the sea. Terpsie marveled at the ocean, having lived so close all her life but never realizing such a thing existed. Nuno delighted in her wonder at new things. He started feeling better about everything.

The first day, they slept under bushes with the sound of the crashing waves below. Nuno was exhausted, struggling to walk half as far as he used to in a night. Terpsie managed to catch two more rabbits for them. As night slowly descended and with a full stomach, he slowly rose to his feet and they continued their journey.

Nuno warned Terpsie, "Tonight, we have to get past that large town ahead of us. If we can't do so before dawn, we'll need to find a place to hide. Every time we pass a potential hiding place, we have to remember it. Might need to backtrack to hide there. Whatever happens, we can't be caught out in the open during the day."

Terpsie nodded her head in agreement but not really understanding as she had never been close to people before. She knew to avoid them, but she was more curious than afraid. There were a few times over the years when hikers would wander by on the trails and see her. All they would do is say to the other hikers, "Hey, look at that pretty kitty hiding in the bushes." Then, they would continue walking away.

Poor Nuno lost his self-confidence after his injury. Besides, he was not a cat. Anyone who looked closely would see his stubby little tail and his big ears. As he was warned by many, if they caught him, he would spend the rest of his life in a strange prison that people called a zoo. He would be a curiosity in a cage. The very thought of that made him shake in fear.

Newport Beach, by the ocean, consists of several islands and peninsulas. For most of the night, they had to walk in the shadows behind buildings surrounded by concrete with few places to hide. They passed restaurants, car dealers, banks, real estate offices, and every other manner of nondescript concrete construction. Having to cross several bridges did not help Nuno's anxiety level. He dared not trust his swimming abilities anymore.

The sun was starting to rise when they finally arrived at the long beach of Huntington Beach. This was the next in a long line of beach towns that would fill the distance to the port of Long Beach, to Los Angeles and further north. That meant there were long beaches

intersected by wharfs and town centers.

Nuno introduced Terpsie to the strange potluck of garbage cans. She did not want to have anything to do with them. Even Nuno had forgotten his distaste for them. But the quick walk through the very urban Newport Beach made them hungry. They found some half-eaten chicken sandwiches. Later they found a drainpipe to hide in during the day.

"Nuno, that was the worst thing I ever ate in my life."

"Dearest, trust me, you will eat far worse before this trip is over."

She sulked at the thought. He fell into a deep sleep, completely exhausted. The next night they only walked for a few hours before Nuno had to rest in another drainpipe. He had not recovered from the day before.

He awoke when Terpsie dropped a large bird in front of him.

"Hey, did you know that the other end of this pipe leads to a large marsh and scrubland area? There I found these fat burrowing owls that live in holes in the ground there. You eat this one. I'll be right back with another one."

"Ah, real food! What would I do without you?"

Nuno relished a fresh dinner. He knew there would probably be no more until they reached Xisto. He hoped that they would quickly find his favorite ship, *California Dreaming,* and not have to wait long. They were only three days into this trip.

So far, Terpsie seemed to have no regrets of leaving their home. Nuno worried that fear would grip her heart like it did with him the first time he saw the thick rope leading from the dock to the ship. Would she refuse to board the ship after he did find it? What would he do then, stay with her or make the voyage alone?

He could not sleep anymore. Dusk was closing in. Soon, Terpsie returned with another burrowing owl. He watched her eat it, lost in thought.

When she finished, she asked, "Hey, why are you so quiet?"

"Oh, it's nothing. I feel better. Thanks for the bird. We probably won't have any more of that until we arrive to Xisto. Let's get going."

"Don't tell me that. And how about giving me some time to digest my meal, please?"

After a while, she got up, and they started the next leg of their journey. They passed many more towns with the word 'Beach' in their names. They only had one dangerous experience.

One day, a man was walking his dog on the beach near the drainpipe where they were sleeping. The dog smelled them and became extremely excited to discover what it was. The man let the dog off his leash, and he came bounding over to their little lair aggressively barking.

"Oh no! A damn dog!" Nuno snarled.

Terpsie arched her back with all her fur standing on end and let out a most fearsome hiss. The man heard the hissing Terpsie.

"What is it, boy? Did you find a cat? Go sic him!" The dog's owner egged him on.

The dog was so close to Terpsie that she could bat his face with her outstretched paw. He was furiously snarling and showing his fangs. Normally, Terpsie would run away, but she knew Nuno could not.

Just when Terpsie's heart was turning from anger to fear, Nuno stepped out from the shadows behind her. He could not hiss, but instead he growled so loud that the dog's owner realized that his dog had found something else besides a cat. Even the dog was confused at the sight of two large cats who should have run away a long time ago, but for some reason were standing their ground.

The dog looked relieved when his owner called him back. "Ah, Butch, come here, boy. I think we better leave whatever that is alone. Let's go." Safely back on his leash, the dog whimpered a bit as they left the scene.

"Oh, how I hate dogs!" Nuno spat the words out. "I hate them worse than bears. You might meet a bear only once in a lifetime. But dogs? They're everywhere!"

"They seem like bullies to me. I understand we must share the same space as coyotes, and they are a threat to us. But we are all just trying to survive in the world of people. But what is it with dogs?"

"They're all fat from living with people. They're not looking for food, just fun. Seems that many of their masters are bullies, too. One dog is not so bad. They're really terrible when they're in groups. Damn things. Fortunately, where we're going, we won't meet them."

They rested for the remaining hours of the day. Nuno could smell the ships at port and knew that they would soon arrive at the point of no return. His doubts of what Terpsie would do when she faced the path onto the ship kept him awake. How would she decide the biggest choice of her life?

CHAPTER EIGHTEEN

Our favorite travelers spent two days at the Seal Beach Nature Reserve, gorging themselves on scrub jays and rabbits. They had one more night left to cross the aptly named beach of Long Beach before arriving at the giant port. Nuno wanted some more time before the fateful decision had to be made. Would she go or not? He was afraid she would not, then what would he do, return without her? Would he?

"Come on, Nuno. Why so glum? You've been silent all day." She asked him after finishing their dinner.

"Oh, nothing. Just tired. That's all."

"No. It's something more than that. Don't tell me you're reconsidering?"

"Reconsidering? No, of course not. Let's get some rest. We have a long night ahead of us."

They stayed in the shadows where the beach met the road to avoid the bright moonlight. There were only a few times when they had to hide to let a late-night jogger or a whimpering dog walker pass. By the time the sun started to rise, they arrived at a protected green space close to the bridge that would take them over to the maze of lagoons, railways, waiting truck lanes, and hundreds of rows of stacked metal containers that is the Port of Long Beach.

Nuno still remembered where *California Dreaming* tied up and where he first stood on the land of the California of his youthful dreams. It was on a spit of land off to the side where the smaller tramp freighters would dock. They passed the areas where the giant oil tankers from Houston, the car carriers from Osaka, and the super freighters carrying all imaginable consumer goods from Shanghai docked.

"This is the spot. This is where I landed all those years ago. It's not here yet. We'll have to wait."

"How do you know it will arrive at the same place?"

"You're right. We'll have to keep a sharp lookout for it. Let's walk to the end of the wharf."

Their ship was indeed not there. Nor was it there the next week or the week after that. In the meantime, they hid in between the nearby rows of containers waiting to be hauled somewhere by truck or train. They searched through the occasional trash can where workers tossed away their meals. They had to be extremely careful as the port operated twenty-four hours a day. But the port workers were always too busy concentrating on their job at hand to notice two small shadows moving carefully along the row of freighters.

One night they had just finished walking along the row of tramp steamers like they did for two and a half weeks already. Still no sign of their ship. Nuno was starting to panic. Maybe they were not at the right place after all. What now?

Just then, Terpsie cried out, "Nuno! Is that it over there? On the other side. See? The third from the left."

Nuno looked long and hard. Finally, he shouted, "Yes, Terpsie! That's it! Let's hurry over there before it leaves!"

They hustled a long way around to the special ship. Nuno moved as fast as his hurt leg would allow. He muttered the whole time, "*No. Please don't leave until we get there.*"

They arrived an hour later, and the ship was still there. It had just arrived, and containers were being pulled from it. Work was slow as tramp freighters were not the highest priority. It was not going anywhere for a while.

Instead of racing to the familiar rope holding the ship secure, Nuno led them to hide under a container mover parked to the side.

"What are we doing here, Nuno?"

"I need to catch my breath before we climb up that long rope onto the ship."

"Of course, that was quite a run to get here. Take your time. I'll go look for food."

"No, stay here. There is plenty of food on board. Let's talk."

"Fine. What about?"

Nuno panted a while longer, waiting for his heart to stop pounding. But it continued pounding even after his breathing calmed down. He could not bear waiting any longer.

"Terpsie, you are about to take a trip that has no return. You will take a long journey to a place that is in many ways much worse than here. I have tried to describe my homeland to you, especially all the reasons why I took the journey here in the first place.

"Once we board this ship, there is no turning back. There is no place for doubts, disappointment, or complaints. If you want to change your mind, this is the time to do it. If you have any fears and decide to head back, I'd understand completely.

"I have been thinking these past few days that if you do decide not to continue, that'd be fine. Yet my heart tells me that I really must return with or without you. It would break my heart and I'd regret it the rest of my life. I can't explain it, Terpsie. Something is compelling me to return. Take your time before you answer."

Terpsie was silent for quite some time considering what he said. Nuno's heart was pounding even harder close to bursting.

Finally, she rose and stood right in front of Nuno with her nose against his. She answered, "I have known many crazy cats in my time, house cats, feral cats, even wild cats. But none of them are as crazy, silly, and sometimes down right maddening as my lynx.

"Yes, you heard that right, my lynx. I've never met anyone who was such a wonderful mate as you. All these years, you were the only one to stay with me and share life's ups and downs, all its joys and sorrows. For the first time, I felt the love and happiness that we hear about in fairy tales.

"I believe you that Xisto is worse than here, even much worse, as you say. But dearest Nuno, know this: I would follow you to the ends of the earth. Even if we were stuck in some human's small apartment or worse in one of their zoos, I would consider it an honor to be by your side. So, stop moping and let's get ourselves up that rope!"

"Oh, Terpsie! That's beautiful!" Nuno replied and then busily licked her face like he would with one of his kittens.

"Now you see that long rope there? We have to climb up that as fast as we can without being noticed or falling into the water."

Terpsie in her excitement was the first up the rope, over the anti-rat barrier, and onto the ship. Nuno hobbled after her and up the rope. But when he came to the anti-rat barrier that he easily leapt over so many times before at every port where he and Figo stopped, he could not pass over it. He tried to climb over but got stuck halfway. He struggled but his paws started to slip from the rope. He looked way down at the water far below. He knew he could not swim anymore. Fear and anger gripped his heart. He did not want to die now that life was going so well again.

Suddenly, two paws gripped his shoulders and yanked him across the barrier. Terpsie had climbed down the rope and rescued the struggling Nuno with her hind claws deeply embedded in the rope.

"You're not going anywhere but with me into this ship. Stop playing around and get up here."

Once safely onboard, Nuno licked her face to show his appreciation and led her to the open hold with the containers below. "Follow me," he said as he leapt down onto the top of one container then onto another one until he reached the bottom. Terpsie followed.

"Now, I'll show you where we sleep and eat." He showed her the best place for sleeping. "This is where Figo and I slept out of sight and away from the oily smells."

He showed her the kitchen. "We'll have to be scavengers for a while. Look, it's the same trash can with the same chicken sandwiches inside!"

He pulled one out and ate the half chicken patty. "Taste just as awful, too. Here, you try."

Terpsie poked it, "Nah, I'm not hungry yet."

They walked around the containers until the sun began to rise. They retired back to their sleeping space. After a few hours, the ship came to life. The engines began their mighty growl, and the ship started to move away from the dock. Terpsie leapt up with a cry.

"Relax, silly. That's only the ship starting its journey." He reassured her.

"Never had the ground move under me like that. Sorry."

"No problem. I was the same. This means that in less than two weeks we'll be there."

They fell back to sleep as the ship left the port and headed out to the open sea. They stirred themselves as the moon rose overhead. Terpsie decided she was hungry enough to eat whatever was in the trash can. As they wandered around the containers, Terpsie stopped and looked up at the stack of containers.

"Nuno, I am thinking of a serious problem that we must solve."

"Oh? What's that?"

"You jumped down here. But after we arrive, how will you jump back up?"

Nuno froze with fear. "Yes, you're right. I never thought of that. Now what will I do? I can't stay trapped on this ship until my dying day!" He started to panic.

"Now, stop that. Panicking will not help anything. I have felt this for a while. I believe that your hip has healed, but your mind has not. Look, we have some time. I want you to jump onto the top of that container. Try it."

Nuno pulled himself together and tried to jump, but he could not reach more than half the way up.

"Looks like we found our nightly activity. You will jump to the top of that container and onto the next one until you can reach the top. How will you take me to Xisto if you can't get off the ship? Let's get going."

Nuno tried for hours each night until he was exhausted, not quite getting to the top. Time was slipping away. The ship only had one more day. Terpsie had to help.

"Look. Watch me." And she easily leapt up to the container's top. "See how easy that is? Now, I want you to focus. Focus on us getting to Xisto. Focus on introducing me to your family and friends. Concentrate!"

Nuno concentrated on leading her down the narrow lynx path to their little village of dens. He thought how he would introduce her to vinho verde and how to dance the fandango. He focused on accompanying her through the hills and forest of his first home. He focused and leapt with his eyes closed. His feet landed on the top of the container next to Terpsie. He did it!

"See? I knew you could do it! Now jump onto the next one."

Nuno could not believe it. He looked up at the next one and jumped on top of that one, too. He jumped up and down the stacks of containers the rest of the night with joy in his heart. He broke through the sorrow that had gripped his heart like a vise. He was like a little lynx cub again.

The ship arrived at the Port of Lisboa. They leapt their way to the top and down the rope. The anti-rat barrier was no longer a problem for Nuno to hop over. Once on dry land, he led her back the way he came so many years before.

Indeed, after ten days, he did lead her down the familiar narrow path to the little lynx village below. Everyone came out and welcomed them with plenty of face lickings all round. The joyous occasion called for the vinho verde and musical instruments to be brought out. Nuno's friends and brothers pulled him to the front of everyone, and they danced the fandango the rest of the night.

FINAL THOUGHTS

Kitten was taken in by the couple who stopped their car. They took her to a new home where she learned the joys of treats and regular meals. She was given a new name: Gwennie, short for Gwendolyn. Later, her life would be full of adventures and voyages of her own. But that, my friends, is a story for another time.

Nuno and Figo thank you very much for reading their story and they trust you enjoyed it. This is the result of many years of work. They ask you, dear reader, to please leave a thoughtful and considerate review on Amazon. These are especially important to the author. The link is below. If CTRl+clicking does not work, please copy and paste it into your browser and you will be taken directly to the book review page.

https://www.amazon.com/review/create-review?asin=1735260622

Also, please leave a review on www.goodreads.com. https://www.goodreads.com/book/show/55336686-the-adventures-of-nuno-and-figo

If CTRl+clicking the link below does not work, please copy and paste it into your browser and you will be taken directly to a landing page on the author's website. When you sign up for the writer's newsletter, you can download some additional content for free like more about Gwennie, who will be the subject of another book, or the latest about the plight of Iberian Lynxes and the organizations trying to save them. You can always unsubscribe later.

https://creative-trailblazer-5290.ck.page

The adventures of Gwennie (Kitten) continue with her own fascinating story to tell. You can follow her in the sequel: The Amazing Tale of Gwennie: Homeless to Palace.

ABOUT THE AUTHOR

Born in Philadelphia, Thomas Murray is foremost a storyteller and has been writing all his life. He was a published member of the San Francisco Poet's Union and winner of Bay Area poetry and short story awards. He currently lives in a palace in Portugal.

Having lived on 5 continents for over 25 years and traveled to 88 countries, he has trained his mind to be sensitive to the wide range of nuances that make up the personalities of everyone he meets. Appreciating global cultures is fundamental to everything he writes. He includes many details about the places and characters to make the readers feel they are part of the story. When he is not writing, he is travelling and learning foreign languages, currently Portuguese.

You can learn more about Thomas and his writing at https://www.thomasmurraywriter.com/

Please like his Facebook page: https://www.facebook.com/thmurraywriter

You can contact the writer at Bastet Publishing: info@bastet.ink

ABOUT THE ILLUSTRATOR

Madalena Bastos is an illustrator, dreamer and inventor from Portugal. Her company, Mariqosa, was born from a cocoon of illustrated ideas, which now flies through the imagination of the young at heart. It opens wings to originality, creating educational games, interactive books and other instruments that encourage creativity.

You can learn more about her work at: www.mariqosa.pt

Also by the Same Author

The Eye of the Beholder, Bastet Publishing, 2020 (first in the Gwendolyn series)

A young art forger on the run …

Gwendolyn, a likable rogue with attitude, is secretly a successful fine-art forger rubbing shoulders with society's elite and shady art dealers. When she switches her painting with the original in a private home and escapes, she is confident with another successful heist. Until the next day when the owners are found murdered.

Framed for murder, she must travel to dangerous exotic lands to find the real murderers and clear her name. But as she delves deeper into the dangerous underworld of art forgery and betrayal, she realizes that she may be in over her head.

As the stakes get higher and her enemies close in, Gwendolyn must use all her cunning and skill to survive. Will she be able to untangle the web of lies and clear her name? Or will she become the next victim in a deadly game of cat and mouse?

https://www.amazon.es/dp/1735260606

Red Is a Color, Bastet Publishing, 2024 (second in the Gwendolyn series)

Is it a crime to be a redhead?

Gwendolyn, our favorite art forger and seductress extraordinaire, returns for another hair-raising adventure. Set in the sensuous backdrop of Portugal, Gwendolyn's latest project starts off as just another painting to forge and another wealthy eccentric to con. But as she delves deeper into the lifestyle of her unsuspecting mark, she begins to uncover more questions than answers.

How did he acquire a previously unknown Renaissance masterpiece by Botticelli? Why does he spend every evening worshipfully gazing at his personal goddess of love? Who is his tempestuous friend with an evil obsession with redheads? Who are the fanatical cultists trailing her every move?

The shadows of reality and myth blur, threatening to swallow her up in a deadly abyss... Will she survive this latest escapade with her life, much less her sanity intact?

www.amazon.com/dp/B0D64LM15C

The Amazing Tale of Gwennie: Homeless to Palace, Bastet Publishing, 2022 (second and last in the Gwennie series)

From homeless cat to palace queen…

How did Gwennie journey from being a forlorn homeless cat in southern California to being the spoiled queen of a palace in Portugal? As the daughter of Nuno, an Iberian Lynx, and Terpsie, a Maine Coon cat, this (mostly) true story continues as the second in the series that started with The Adventures of Nuno and Figo: The Incredible Journey of Two Unlikely Friends (Illustrated). Gwennie travels to even more exotic places than her famous father. Follow her journey as she incredibly ends up in Portugal, the same country as her father's homeland, a half a world away.

https://www.amazon.es/dp/B0BCS7NNBX

Only After Dark: One Man's Descent into Obsession and Madness, Bastet Publishing, 2021

Prepare to be enthralled by a dark and beguiling world as an American author of horror discovers an alluring and mysterious existence beyond his own in the post-Revolution Portugal of the late 1970s. Running from his past, he moves into an abandoned crumbling palace, eager to make progress on his next bestselling novel. A chance encounter with an unnamed, yet shockingly sensual woman pulls aside the veil of the world to reveal an alluring existence defined by unnatural delights and mind-twisting hedonism.

As his mysterious lover draws him further into her realm of shadows and ultimate pleasure, how much is he willing to sacrifice to keep her? And will there be anything left of his sanity when his would-be goddess is through with him? A tale told in the vein of Lovecraft and Edgar Allen Poe, this book will have you on the edge of your seat and wanting more.

https://www.amazon.es/dp/1735260673

Ponce de León: A Modern Sequel, Bastet Publishing, 2022

What is the meaning of life if you can live forever?

What if 500 years ago Ponce de León did discover the Fountain of Youth? He and his crew have everything anyone could dream of: wealth, health, love of friends, and time; eternal time. But is immortality a blessing or a curse? Ponce de Léon is not so sure. He enters a personal crisis seeking this answer to the meaning of life. His search for answers leads him to a truth he never expected.

https://www.amazon.es/dp/173526069X